PORTAL

ELDON CROWE

Portal
Copyright © 2018 by Eldon Crowe

All rights reserved. No part of this publication may be reproduced, distributed, or transmitted in any form or by any means, including photocopying, recording, or other electronic or mechanical methods, without the prior written permission of the author, except in the case of brief quotations embodied in critical reviews and certain other non-commercial uses permitted by copyright law.

Tellwell Talent
www.tellwell.ca
ISBN
978-0-2288-0765-0 (Paperback)

For my mother, whose happy greeting
and love will always be missed,
And for Chris, Mr. 'SCI-FI.'

I

She pushed out into the hall and the wooden-slatted floor was hard beneath her padded feet. There were no lights and only the vaguest hints of doors along the bare walls. *This is not the hallway of the small house in Tusten Hills.*

"You shouldn't go out there," said the girl through the open doorway behind her.

She let out a ragged breath. *I am Dr. Mariss Arlen Keppeler. I was born October 12, 2087, in Tusten Hills, Iowa. I am 42 years old.*

A fluorescent light snapped on somewhere overhead, throwing a sickly, cobalt hue over the world – at least, the world as it had become for her.

"You need to rest," said the girl, plaintively, in her sister's voice, "I want you to *rest.*"

"Like hell," she mumbled. Stepping forward, a wave of vertigo washed over her and she shot a hand toward the wall. A garbled cry escaped her parched lips. It *gave*. For an instant her hand had sunk into it as if it were pudding. "Oh, God," she muttered, "Oh, *God."* Tentatively, she reached to touch it again; give it a quick rap with her knuckles. This time it resounded solidly. *And this is not a wall.* She laughed; a high, frenetic bark. "I am Dr. Mariss Keppeler," she shrilled into the hallway and she cursed the terror that constricted her throat. *You are a respected doctor of radio-astronomy, not a hysterical child. Calm yourself and THINK.*

She looked up along the ceiling, an indistinct, grey strip before the dull, blue light. In the instant, another fluorescent winked on, farther along, buzzing softly. "I am Dr. Mariss *Arlen* Keppeler and this is not my childhood home in Tusten Hills, Iowa - in which I lived from the age of 2 until the Launch." She lurched forward on unsteady legs. They throbbed with a dull, yet insistent pain. Her feet were chilled to the bone and her head swam.

Abruptly, she realized that she was wearing the flannel pajama onesie of her girl-hood – now grown to adult proportions - with the mark of her father's Syndicate emblazoned upon the left breast. *Absurd!* Indeed, the primary legacy of her family, which had always warmed and comforted her when she was a child, seemed to be profoundly out of place here, now, in the midst of this lie - the very place where it should most belong.

"And that girl," she croaked, stumbling painfully along the cold passage. "That -" She cleared her throat and licked her dry lips, "that *thing* behind me…..in that bedroom with the twin beds and a stuffed rabbit with one ear missing and brown *teddy* bears on the walls is *NOT* Solea Tusten Arlen. My sister." She began to sob. *Damn it!* Her vision doubled, then trebled.

A light, a third one – this one a soft, butter yellow – grew slowly out of the dimness ahead.
"Oh." She stopped, sniffling, and looked with wide eyes.

"I am in," she said in a low, tremulous voice, "a hallucinatory, mental state. Very likely, I am being restrained and sedated against my will."
Slowly, she slid a covered foot forward and kicked a green balloon into the air over a rustic, oaken floor. A single balloon. She glanced up. Rich, elm-panelled ceiling. "My parietal lobe and very likely my hippocampus are being stimulated by an external source." *It was his idea. The balloon. So it wouldn't be only a tragedy. But a hope too.* She panned her eyes slowly around the softly-lit, sparsely-decorated room. There was not a sound. *It's the kitchen. I'll be damned. It's the kitchen the day of…..the day when…..*Her eyes fell on the balloon on the floor again. She licked her lips and tasted the faintest hint of blood this time. She took in a faint breath. "I am being manipulated into re-living images," she murmured, "Images from my p-"
A tremor coursed through the floor and ran up through her feet into her body, almost pitching her

forward onto her face. The balloon stirred upon the floor. The soft, yellow light flickered. *What in the hell was that now? What is going on?*

"What do you want from me?" she screamed, wiping a tear angrily from her cheek with a flannelled sleeve. Abruptly, she went and seized the green balloon in her hands. "Don't you know that you're killing me?" she insisted to the room, "Wherever I am, wherever you have me, I am in a state of advanced dehydration." She was panting now, her breath rattling through her dry chest. She brandished the balloon in shaking hands and tilted her head toward the ceiling. "And why this day, huh? It was the saddest and yet the most precious day of my life."

She dropped the balloon and her arms fell limply to her sides.

Slowly, gently, the balloon drifted down and bounced idly upon the oaken floor.

"My God," she whispered, "I'm in Limbo."

II

"Mariss."

Another moan escaped her brittle lips. She whirled, heart in throat. "Dad?"

He sat at the kitchen table, the sleeves of his soiled coveralls rolled up past the elbows. His tall, lanky frame leaned forward, his thin arms half-raised. His long, narrow fingers clutched gleaming, metal tools. "Come and help me with this," he said. His voice was sand-paper.

She regarded him, frowning. She tried to affect a calm she did not feel even though, inside, her heart was knocking against her ribs. Desperately, she forced herself to breathe deeply. *They got this part right, at least. Besides the balloon. You were working on something that night. Dad. If that really is what you are. This night. Something you finished. Something you promised the Collective the Syndicate would complete by the Launch. The very night Mom and I left.*

Slowly, silently, eyes narrowed warily at the intent, down-turned face of the corporeal figure seated at the table, she stepped across the wooden floor. The balloon had fled. Now there was only him.

She stood at the table.

"It's almost finished," her father said, "It needs only one more thing, a touch."

She shivered, still staring hard at his face. Her eyes sought in vain to render every detail of it for it seemed to fade and waver even as she looked at it. "Why didn't you come, Dad?" she whispered. *Why didn't you follow? You paved the way. You made it possible for what was left of us to survive – and even to go beyond.*

The faint, musky smell of him, the slight sweatiness of his coveralls when he worked in them was all around her. The tools clicked together. Gently, they nudged and scraped something that sat in front of him.

Forcing her eyes from him, she turned them slowly to the object upon the table. It was odd that she had not noticed it before. It was small, no larger than a loaf of bread, yet it was strangely formless. Its surface was a dull grey which held no shine or sheen beneath the soft, yellow light that still emanated from the ceiling, and studding its indiscernible skin were what looked like small, black knobs. Her frown deepened. "Wait," she murmured, "That's not right."

She watched as the tool in her father's right hand traced small, counter-clockwise circles upon the object's grey skin. It had a sharp point yet made hardly a sound and left no trace of its movement upon the dull, grey surface.

"You were working," she began, slowly, trying to plumb her thoughts amidst the thick haze which surrounded them, trying to go back, "on a mass, spectral, field emitter. An array."

Now the left-hand tool stirred, brushing a wide, shallow, flexible snout across the object's left side. The formless surface seemed to glitter slightly where it touched.

She frowned again, watching the tools, watching the hands that held them. "You had a theory," she murmured, languidly, ".....something the Collective wanted *so* badly to be true....."

He was setting down one of the tools now and adjusting one of the myriad, black knobs upon the object's top. She saw it turn slightly in his rough, callused hand.

"We were desperate," she said and now her voice was a low groan. "Yes. It was only the beginning. We could not live up on the Network indefinitely. We had a food-source and energy....." - She shook her head - ".....but it wasn't enough. None of it was enough. In another generation – very soon now - we would all be dead, whether we were left on the cruel surface or not. Unless....." Her breath gave a hitch in her throat and she stared so hard at the object upon the table that there was nothing else now. "…..Unless we could go beyond. Your theory was correct, Dad – we *could* go beyond. But first you had to find the key to the door."

The hands stopped.

Light-headed, trembling, she continued to stare at the formless thing sitting before her eyes.

But that's not what this is. This is not the array. This is not what you were working on, Dad. It's wrong. It almost reminds me of…..

"Only one more touch, Marisseena," said her father, in a strange, wooden voice, "and it is done."

She started violently, darting her eyes to him.

He held out to her a tool. And the hand stretched out toward her was thin and gnarled and ancient, its skin sallow and mottled.

She leapt back, stumbling over her own feet. "Who are you?" she screamed. She goggled at him in horror. "You are not my father," she shrilled. "My father, Dr. Markus Alben Arlen remained behind, on the irradiated surface. He *died* within seven years of the Launch! He was strong and hale; in the midst of his prime. And in the midst of his stubbornness. He died trying to help all those who were too sick to leave."

The hand trembled, still reaching towards her, the implement in its curled fingers shaking. "Marisseena," whispered the old man.

Her hands flew to her head and she clutched at her short, dark, matted hair. "And don't *call* me that! Only my father called me that. Not now. Not like this.

There's something wrong, something very wrong, can't you see that? I have to figure it out." A violent shaking took hold of her and the terror in her was like a hot iron now, twisting and writhing inside her gut. *If I'm dead, this isn't Limbo. It's hell.*

The man at the table sat in shadows even though the yellow light still shone down upon him, upon them both. "It needs your touch and no other," he croaked. "You must remember."

Remember? Remember what? How to fix your own bloody machine?

No, another machine…..Another…..

The kitchen around her began to spin. Her breath, which was the only sound, came to her ears as a wheezing rattle from her lungs and she thought, suddenly, of the dying elephant she'd seen on the view-monitor at home before the Launch, lying helplessly upon the wasted, withering savannah of southern Africa in its own blood and vomit. It too had been wheezing just like she was now, every breath an agony. She had never thought of it since that moment. Never. Until now. Until she had ended up here.

And just as it had done when she had been only a child, not understanding why any of this should be, her strength left her and she had to reach out and steady herself on the edge of the table.

"The Collective brought my father's body up to the Network," she gasped through chapped lips, "and there was a funeral, the biggest funeral that there ever was." She was crying openly now just like she had when she had been eight, watching the elephant die on the Earth-wide link, but this time there were no tears. They had all dried up. Her heart was like a red, hot brand within her chest. "He was 42 years old – the same as me."

Her legs gave out beneath her and she fell hard to the wooden floor. There was a buzzing in her ears and the kitchen swam above her.

The man at the table rose slowly and ponderously and, dimly, she heard him stumble against it. "Mariss," he groaned, "You must remember. You must fix it."

And suddenly, lying on the long-ago, oaken floor of her family's long-ago Iowa home, she knew him.

No. It cannot be! How? HOW?

III

The girl, wearing a flannel onesie marked with brown teddy bears, stood in the doorway. She looked, petulantly, across the kitchen at the woman lying unconscious upon the oaken floor beside the table. The soft, yellow light from the ceiling cast the sunken eye-sockets of the old man standing beside the table in shadow. His thin arms hung limply at his sides.

"I told it to rest," *said the girl, peevishly,* "but it wouldn't. And now look what's happened. It's not doing it." *The man swayed on his feet, breathing faintly, his eyes cast down upon the figure on the floor. He whispered something. The girl padded across the room and stood over the unconscious woman. She half-raised her small hands and closed her eyes.* "I can still feel it," *she said,* "It's strong." *Taking a deep breath, she opened her eyes. The man began murmuring softly to himself. Looking side-ways at him, her long, black hair with its odd, metallic sheen, hanging across her small face, the girl said:* "You still see what it saw?"

The man did not meet her piercing, translucent, yellow-green eyes but continued to look, rather, at the inert woman. "Yes," *he said, nodding slowly.*

"But you do not know it."

He looked up for a moment and, with a long sigh, panned his bleary, sunken eyes about the room. His withered body seemed to wilt. "No," *he whispered.*

The girl's spiral-shaped pupils swallowed her lime-yellow irises. "You were supposed to know," *she said in a deep, hoarse growl. The man blanched and stumbled backward against the chair, sitting awkwardly upon it once more.* "Please," *he whimpered,* "It has been too long. And I did not know her then…..It was the wrong time."

"Be quiet!" *screamed the girl. He let out another whimper and sat sullenly, looking down at the woman again.*

The girl did the same and slowly her opaque eyes cleared and became translucent once more. She cocked her head. "Mah – Ree – See – Nah," *she said.*

The man sat, watching, breathing raggedly.

"Why does it not like that…..name?" *said the girl.*

"Her father -" *he gasped.*

The dark spirals in the girl's eyes flared again. "Father." *She spat the word. Looking down at herself, she placed her small hands over her stomach, spreading her fingers over the flannel.*

Her breath came faster and she grimaced. "Sister," *she groaned, as if in pain. Opening her luminous eyes again, she turned them fiercely upon the old man and he fairly quaked in his chair.* "Huzz-Band," *she growled.* "What are these? Tell me!"

Carefully keeping his own gaze down upon the unconscious woman, he said, tremulously, "They are not names – our personal 'designations.' They….. signify who we are…..to one other."

Abruptly, the girl turned and stepped toward him. He cowered back in his chair.

She stood at the table and looked down at him. His averted gaze was drawn to her strange eyes like iron filings to a magnet.

He gasped. "No," *he said, feebly,* "Why do you do this to me? Why do you torture me?"

"Creatures," *spat Dr. Mariss Arlen Keppeler, twenty years younger and with long, dark hair. She cupped the old man's shaking chin in her hand, her lime-yellow eyes gripping his dark, rheumy ones. He gawped up at her.*

"Please," *he whispered.* "Not like this. Not like this."

"You are all foolish creatures. I must know. I must know now!" *Her eyes darkening, she cocked her head at him.*

He gasped again. "You already know it all," *he groaned,* "Everything. Even what I had forgotten." *He raised a bony hand and tapped a gnarled, shaking finger to the side of his head.* "You can look in here all you want, see every moment. I don't care anymore. It is the bond that we shared. Because this woman lying on the floor and I -"

The girl-turned-woman standing before him flashed her up-raised hands towards him and he broke off with a shudder, open-mouthed.

"I do not care about these useless bonds," *she hissed,* "You do not know what it is. And you could not get this one to make it work either. Look down at it again and this time you will see it as it is - not as this one on the floor saw it. It could not see it properly."

The man shivered, blinking. Taking a quick gulp of air, he tore his blood-shot eyes from hers and lowered them to the table.

The object lay atop it. Changed.

At that moment, another tremor moved beneath them, this time rippling the very oaken slats of the floor. The yellow light in the ceiling flickered again and dust sifted down from the elm panels above them.

The young woman, eyes still black, gave a snarl of frustration and for an instant her face shifted. The nose and mouth slid partially across it as if it were wax. Her hands, still raised, became misshapen lumps of white dough. The man let out a pitiable cry. And then it was gone. Everything was as it was.

"Tell me if you know it in its true shape," *said the woman through clenched teeth,* "and I will not destroy you. You think that you are still protected but now I have the other one. It could not see it right but soon -"

The object on the table broke in, cutting her off:

"Dr. Keppeler. Dr. Keppeler. Are you awake? The tremors in this region are slowly increasing in frequency and in intensity. It must be of the highest priority that you locate the others if they are still alive and attempt the return as quickly as possible for I fear that you may be in danger. But I need you to make contact. If I continue to receive no input from you, my protocols require me to activate Lock-Out Status and enter Hibernation Mode."

The young woman swung her up-raised hands toward the object, no longer a dull, grey box.

The old man, entirely forgotten, wilted once more, slumping in his chair.

"I feel nothing in you," *whispered the false woman to the object, closing her eyes,* "and yet you speak. But not with words, with sounds only. Teach me these sounds. Teach me….. please."

IV

Dr. Mariss Arlen Keppeler awoke.

Two sensations greeted her. There was darkness. She looked around her, knowing that she had opened her eyes, yet there was nothing to be gained by it, certainly no understanding of where she was. She *felt* the maw around her for it was not merely a complete absence of light but an actual physical touch; it blanketed her as a cocoon, immersing her in its arms. And there was a fading, yet still vivid, pounding inside her head. Indeed, for an unguessed length of time it was all she could do to lie where she was, her thoughts so thick and sluggish that they could find no solid footing.

But there was a sound.

Soft. Continuous. She concentrated upon it. It was comforting, helping her to steady her mind and to ease the throbbing within her head. It was familiar and natural and she closed her eyes, listening to it for a long while.

A waterfall.

Her eyes snapped open. There was still only the dark. She took in a deep breath but at once her chest spasmed painfully. She coughed, dryly, her sternum aching. The air felt chill and damp. But invigorating. She felt strength come back into her arms and she lifted her right slowly from her side. It tingled from her finger-tips to her shoulder yet felt as if it were made of solid plasteel.

No, not a waterfall. A trickle.

Now the left. She lifted it and turned it, her muscles stiff as cords. It required an effort to lay it upon her chest, very carefully, next to her right. She felt a damp, sweat-stained shirt beneath her hands and over her strangely spent body.

What's happened to me? Where am I? Where would there be a trickle of water? Why can I not THINK?

There was a drip - a drip in amongst the sound of the gently falling water. It was odd that she had not noticed it before. A shiver went through her.

I am in a cave.

"Help me," she said but her ears heard only a harsh rasping sound which seemed to resonate around her as in the inside of a drum. *Is that my voice?* Suddenly, the sound of the water was an agony. *I will die soon if I can't get any. I am seriously de-hydrated.* She struggled to sit up, the muscles in her chest and diaphragm screaming, but then froze, an icy sweat breaking out on her forehead and sticking the sleeves of her shirt to her arms. *Someone is watching me.*

"Who's there?" she called out into the blackness and this time she heard her own words but the sound of her voice was an inhuman, guttural croak.

There was no answer but the water.

"I am thirsty," she whispered, "Please."

A faint, scraping sound, as if something slid along a surface, echoed around her and a shaft of dazzling, blue light blazed down from above, stabbing through her eyes and into her skull. She groaned, feebly, bringing her trembling arms up over her face. Her breath was rattling inside her chest, her lungs on fire. Dimly, she was aware of dull, featureless, grey rock all around her, a great, open room as if scooped out of the inside of a mountain.

And, in an instant, she was also aware of its intelligent design.

My God, it's Carlsbad - the Staging Level. Have I been Evac-ed? And from what? Think! Something has gone wrong, very wrong, back on the Network. What else makes sense? She felt her heart straining within her sweat-stained shirt.

She had to remember. She had to remember everything right now. Her life at the very least was in peril, perhaps the lives of many, many more already were. Had she not been assigned to a mission?

She wracked her brain and felt the dull pain inside her head flare. "Beta-One," she whispered into the dead, chill air. "I was part of Beta-One." *I was Beta-One.*

There had been no sign or contact of any kind from Alpha – from Brayton. She remembered that now. For ten months, the Transit Program had been side-lined while the suits and coats had argued over lack of vital resources and probable time lags Beyond. Beta had been a compromise, much smaller on the consumables and resources but still timely enough, it was hoped, to discover or to determine what had happened to Alpha and, if necessary, to complete its mission.

Yet Beta would not have happened at all unless she had come forth and volunteered for it. She could remember, suddenly, going to Idris personally and arguing passionately for it. And, well, being the Founder's daughter had not hindered her chances, nor her own substantial credentials.....

Yet now Beta had failed too, hadn't it? That was quite obvious. It had failed.....and that meant..... "We will never know what happened on the other side," she croaked aloud in the vault-like cavern. "We'll all die."

Her throat constricted in terror and she felt her eyes bulge in their sockets as if to burst clear out of them.

No. Wait. Think about it now. Carlsbad was partially sealed after the Inundation, wasn't it? She heard her own strangled breath wheezing desperately inside the cave. *The World Council thought that the lowest levels would be viable afterward in an emergency, yes, but the Collective shut the whole thing down almost before it began, calling it a misappropriation of vital resources. Everything from that moment on went towards the Launch, didn't it? There were no more attempts at Sub-Terra Fail-Safes. It was the last hopeless act of the failed W.C.* She felt her hairs stand out all over her body in the chill air. *Carlsbad is a No-Go.*

But then where the hell am I?

Drink.

She started violently. Someone had spoken to her. But not aloud. She shuddered again. They were inside her head, whoever was watching her, *what*ever was watching her.

Over there. Beside you. You'll see it.

She clutched her head in trembling hands. She felt very weak. Slowly, grimacing, she sat up and looked beside her.

There was a trough of stone hewn out of the rock at her left elbow and it was filled with clear water. She gave a moan and turned herself on her side. Or tried to. Her legs felt as if they were two dead-falls in a forest; they were unresponsive, lifeless. Ignoring them in her dire need, she twisted her body as best she could and scooped her cupped hands into the trough. She brought the cool water, dripping, to her lips. Sighing in pleasure, she felt it there on her chapped lips and tongue and then gently down her constricted throat. *Not too much too soon. Easy.* She took a few more sips and began to breathe more steadily and more deeply. "Ohh," she moaned, raggedly, "That's better."

She passed a hand down over her face and then wet it again in the trough, running it through her hair, which felt as limp and lifeless as her legs.

It's not Carlsbad and it sure as hell isn't anywhere on the Network. And as much as I want to believe it IS hell I know it isn't that either.

Though there was still what felt like a great, yawning maw inside her head, a sudden and inexorable conclusion forced its way into it.

"Beta did not fail," she murmured, "At least not yet. I'm still through the god-damned Portal."

V

They fled.

Whoever had been watching her, whoever had been inside her head, at that very instant, they weren't there anymore. "I don't understand," she said into the cavern, amidst the sound of the falling and trickling water. "Where am I? Why am I here? And how *long?*"

She looked down at her legs for the first time. "Oh, my God."

Dr. Newton Idris in a white jacket suddenly loomed before her in her still hazy mind's eye. The smell of clinical sterility and the dazzle of the white walls within the External Policy Sector of the Network suddenly assaulted her as they thrust themselves up around her, ghost-like, making her nostrils flare and her eyes squint. The Syndicate had just begun to experiment with induced hyper-sleep, a controlled, gradual lowering of the body's internal temperature after one had been safely sedated. It was not known what time factors or environment or hazards might await successful Transitors beyond the Doorway and so the Sleep had been ordered developed by the Company. It had all been conducted under the watchful eye of Idris, who had taken over the reins of the Syndicate - grown to all-encompassing authority up on the Network once the Collective had yielded control over E. P. He had been only an intern during her father's reign - she could scarcely remember - but had quickly established himself in the company's forefront after the untimely and unexpected departure of the Founder. *Along with Brayton. He was an intern too. Before I met him on the Network. I hadn't wanted anything to do with Admin, only Radio-Astronomy. That was Dad's field and mine. But Brayton was too jock-ish for all that, wasn't he? He wanted the real glory. That's why he volunteered…..for Alpha…..*

She took a ragged breath and placed her hands down upon the congealed substance that covered her legs. It's what had reminded her of the Sleep. Basically, the Sleep started with the goo - 'Space Goo' the techs affectionately called it. It was a conducting gel, very thick, with a high boiling point *as well* as a low freezing point, a wonder, really, of science, itself. Idris's magnum opus and perhaps truly an achievement worthy of placing him exactly where he was – squarely, in the Director's chair.

The water trickled around her, the blue light continued to sting her eyes, and her legs were held fast within Space Goo so thick as to be opaque. *But only my legs. It doesn't make sense.* It was a conductor, she knew, a facilitator of the flow of nutrients to the body during Sleep, helping the on-board computer of the spacecraft to regulate and preserve all of the vitals of the Sleeper. *Yet I was dying of dehydration. Whoever put me here and dunked my legs in it didn't know enough about it.*

Or discovered something about it that we hadn't. The halucinations?

Suddenly, an irrational terror seized her. Screaming, she dug her fingers into the opaque substance smothering her legs and began to gouge small troughs out of it, flinging it wildly through the chill air. "Get it off me! Get it off me!" Her screams echoed loudly off the walls of curving rock and went out, far out, it seemed, beyond them.

You need to rest.

"Fuck you!" she screamed into the cavern. "I'm not resting. I'm not being a poor, sick subject of your demented illusions anymore. Do you understand me?"

With a shriek, she pulled her bare, pale, right leg from its prison. Amazingly, the substance began suddenly to fall to powder in her hands, dry and palely translucent. "Ugh," she said, brushing off her leg and then rubbing her hands together. She found she could lift her left leg out of the congealed gel all by itself and she vigorously brushed it clean as well. Then, panting, heart pounding, she glanced around the cavern.

She lay within a carved depression in the rock, reminding her, unpleasantly, of a funeral bier. Glistening walls of that same, impenetrable, grey rock surrounded her apart from one shadow off from her left foot. The roof was high, perhaps four times her height, she judged, and the shaft of light was coming from a great rent in the stone, like a crack, almost directly above her head. It still hurt her eyes to look near it and when she did it took them a while to re-accustom to the dimmer level of the floor.

"I'm getting out of here," she announced suddenly beneath the harsh, blue light stabbing from the ceiling and amidst the sound of the moving water.

In only her underwear and sweat-stained undershirt, then, she attempted to extricate herself from her stone bed. Her muscles, though now awakened and moving, showed every sign of a very slight atrophy and this again brought to her mind how long she had been in this place – and to what purpose.

"I got to find the Scout, find my coveralls," she said to herself as calmly as she could but aloud so that she could keep down the icy panic that threatened to engulf her. "If my suit isn't needed, I'll just get to the surface, take my bearings. Alpha's signature is out there somewhere, Brayton's out there. I know he is."

Shakily, she stood and swayed upon her own two, bare feet upon the cold, rock floor. *But no onesie? What a pity. It would've been so nice and cozy warm.*

A terrifying cackle burst from her still-chapped lips.

She was losing it.

"Think!" she screamed, seizing her head in her shaking hands, "Focus your mind!" But she could not. She could not even remember - not coming here, not what happened before coming here, not even passing through that mysterious Doorway that her father had somehow jimmied open with his spectral field signals coming from that improbable, strange object that had so fascinated her as a child.

Object? Her hands pounded on her head. The dark region of her mind felt like a chasm whenever she thought along these lines. She could feel the rawness of it – almost as if she had undergone a mental excision. She shuddered. "I'm not your experiment anymore," she said, hoarsely, to the cavern. Lowering her arms, she began to lurch across the floor – and clear through the opening in its hard, glistening walls that had been only a shadow from her stone bed.

Her first thought was, *"It is a waterfall."*

Beyond the cavern where she had lain, there was a vast, long tunnel running to her left and right and it was high, high, yet perilously narrow – she would scarcely be able to travel along it with both arms half-held out from her sides. And coming in a loud, glorious cascade from its high ceiling and sliding down along its far wall into a rent in the side of its floor was a waterfall, a true waterfall.

She laughed again but this time for sheer joy. She could feel the faint, cool spray upon her face and arms. Taking in a deep, cleansing breath, she felt, at once, much of her strength return. Indeed, with each wonderful gulp of that cool air, it felt as if it were re-doubling.

Go back to the place prepared for you. Quickly!

So, they hadn't left her for good, had they? She laughed again into the enlivening, strength-building mist coming off the wonderful, falling water. She held out her hands and let the refreshing coolness flow through her fingers and tilted her head back, letting the mist fall upon her face.

It's not safe for you out there. It's beyond the protected place.

Mariss Arlen Keppeler laughed aloud. "You're afraid!" she shouted over the water, "You're afraid that I might become strong again, that I might figure everything out." She laughed again, loving the sound it made, loving the ability to make it. "And I will."

After yet another deep, invigorating breath, she began to feel light-headed once more, but this time not within some twisted illusion. The waterfall and the mist were *real.* And they were intoxicating as well as rejuvenating. "It's amazing," she said, her head

swimming, "What is this place? It's not Earth…..
and not Limbo. It's better." She began to breathe
faster, making her head spin even more. "We can
live here! We can leave the Network behind. It's
breaking down, running out. But we can live here -"

The floor of the tunnel shook with a thunderous
sound and the falling water leapt out at her, dousing
her head and leaving her gasping and reeling. She
lost her footing and fell to the floor, soaked and
chilled and dazed. Pebbles and stones dislodged
from the ceiling and descended in a shower all over
her, forcing her to cover her head with her hands.

At once, a sharp, cracking sound assaulted her
ears and, behind her, inside the scooped out stone
cavern in which she had awoken, the shaft of blue
light winked out.

She was plunged back into the darkness, wet
and cold, amidst the falling water.

Does that mean my so-called protection is gone?
Her heart throbbed in her ears and her breath pistoned in and out of her lungs amidst the sound of
the water. Her head tilted this way and that. *Am I
alone now? Did it leave me for good?*

"I don't need you," she shouted into the darkness,
"I'll find my Scout. I'll go back. I'll get the others,
all of us, everyone left back on the Network, and
bring them here. We'll live *outside* your cold, slimy
protected area. In the beautiful air. Away from *you!*"

She gasped. *But what about Brayton? Is he really
here too? Or was he just a part of the illusion? He
was so OLD.*

A pin-prick of light caught her eye. Far, far away to her right along the darkened passage, there was a single, tiny source of light. She turned her face toward it. "It's the surface," she whispered, "I know it is. Maybe he's gone out there. My Brayton. My real husband, not some crazy illusion perverted by time. Maybe he's out there right now."

Hesitantly, slowly, she rose from the stone floor of the tunnel, her head spinning in earnest now and the world – whatever world it was – turning beneath her. She regained her feet and held out both arms against the cold, slick, stone walls to steady herself. She was near to the dark maw of the cavern whence she had emerged for she could feel the slightly cooler air within it against her damp face. Evidently the cracking noise had snuffed out its light but not closed its opening.

She faced, resolutely, toward the pin-prick of light once more and began to step toward it. Pebbles and stones jabbed at the bottoms of her feet as she lurched forward and at once she thought of her strange illusion. "The floor was cold there too," she said amidst the sound of the moving water behind her, "down the hall to the yellow light."

Her fingers trailed along damp, stone walls. They were smooth and without crack or line or uneven surface; flawless. "A piece of art," she said, head still swimming, "I must give *that* to my hidden host with the wonderful voice. If it really made this place." She continued on, carefully. "Maybe you found this place, huh?" she cried out into the tunnel, and she heard her voice echo behind her and drift away to nothingness before her. She kept her eyes fastened upon that distant point of light. "Maybe you drove the previous owner mad too!" She laughed again.

She stepped on a jagged piece of stone.

Crying out, hoarsely, she stumbled to her knees. Clutching her foot, cursing, sitting on the stone floor, she groaned feebly. Abruptly, she became aware that her head had stopped spinning, though whether or not as a result of the sudden, shooting pain, she could not tell. The point of light at the end of the passage had grown to the size of a window now, hanging tantalizingly before her eyes. Within it, beyond it, bathed in a blinding, lapis light, lay a small slice of the strangest and most fascinating land-scape she had ever seen. She sat for a while, trying to soothe the throbbing pain in her foot and then struggled to her feet once more, gasping.

"My God, "she whispered, panting, staring, "Like the mesas and canyons of Arizona. Only…..blue."

The sound of the waterfall was faint behind her now. She continued on, gazing in wonder at the ever-widening doorway before her. *A doorway to a new world, a world to which Dad found a way and where the remnants of a dying one can find a new home. It's a…..miracle.*

There was a wheezing, coarse and rasping, filling her ears now. "A new future," she gasped, her throat hitching, "a new life -"

She lay on the stone floor, slowly writhing her arms and legs. Faint gurgling and croaking sounds filled her ears. Her lungs were on fire. It felt as if someone had thrown a thick blanket over her head and was holding it over her mouth and nose with all their strength, trying to strangle her, waiting for all the air inside her body to dissipate.

But I can still see. The light is still there.

Dark spots danced before her eyes, threatening to block it out.

She strained her head, her body convulsing now, turning her eyes up, up above her for the light had moved directly over her head for some strange reason. So close over her head. She saw moving, tattered, blue clouds passing through it.

I can…..touch them.

Dimly, she saw a wildly shaking hand reaching, reaching toward the light.

A cloud, this one very dark, dipped low towards her.

"*Marisseena,*" it whispered.

VI

The water was back. Its gentle sound seemed to caress her faintly throbbing ears. The darkness enfolded her like a shroud, just as it had in the cavern.

"Breathe," said a paper-dry voice, nearby, "You must breathe."

Her throat hitched and she coughed violently. Her lungs seemed as if they were deflated and did not want to open. She flailed her right arm up, clawing desperately at her throat.

"*Slowly!* You must breathe slowly." She felt a hand, trembling in its own right, grasp her arm firmly and yet gently lower it from her face.

She took in a slow, shallow breath, her chest still afire, and then took in another, slightly deeper. She could feel blessed cool air enter into her lungs once more.

"Yes," said the voice, more softly, "That is the way." It was incorporeal, rising out of the blackness. Yet it was familiar.

"Who are you?" she murmured over the water.

She felt the hand let go her arm. "Oxygen," said the voice, "Yes. Oxygen is what you require. It is here.....in this place."

She did not speak further. Rather, she concentrated on her breathing, gently increasing and deepening it. The beating of her heart seemed to fill the tunnel. Yet, gradually, she knew, she was recovering. "I was asphyxiating," she murmured, breathing steadily now, "How could I have been so stupid?"

"Here," said the voice, after a while, and she started as she felt a hand grasp her right forearm and urge her to her feet, "you must come with me now."

There was a brilliant flash of blue light and she cried out in surprise, hastily throwing her arm up over her eyes and stumbling out of the hand's grasp.

"Ah, yes," he murmured, "The light will hurt your eyes. I should have warned you."

She lowered her arm and, having gone to one knee, tentatively squinted up at her ancient husband through the fierce, blue light that now illuminated a thin cross-section of the stone tunnel around them. The crags of his lined face were in its shadow and it was blazing forth from a tube that he clutched in his bony, right hand and which did not waver or gutter but shone steadily; like a beacon.

"Brayton," she croaked, her voice catching, "is it really you or are you still only a dream?"

He reached out his other hand and with surprising strength grasped her shoulder and helped her back to both feet. Her shirt was still damp with water and sweat and she was dimly aware of the omnipresent pebbles beneath her bare feet. She gave a shiver.

"Come," he said, "you will need warmth. Your body temperature is too low."

Silently, shivering slightly, she let him guide her along the passage, away from both the invigorating waterfall and the distant, strange, blue sky beyond the end of the tunnel. They moved deeper into the mountain – if mountain it was.

He went slowly and carefully, his left hand still grasping her right forearm and his right holding out before him the luminous tube of blue light. Glancing down, she noticed that he wore form-fitting, above the ankle, foot-wear of a kind she had never before seen. It looked to be made of a soft, pliable, white material, like silk, yet seemed sturdy enough whenever he trod upon a stone lying on the tunnel floor. She saw that he was clad in a long, flowing robe of the same material, making him look stately, even regal. She gave out the softest snicker. *Brayton? Regal? Not the Brayton I know. Not my jock husband.*

Beneath her very feet, deep, deep below, there came a tremor. Dust sifted down from the ceiling upon them and she felt his hand tighten slightly upon her arm.

They passed several, black maws sunken into both walls along the long, silent, narrow tunnel. Indeed, apart from the receding waterfall behind them, there seemed to be no other, single, moving, living, breathing thing in all this strange world.

The enormity of where she was forced itself down upon her without warning.

Her heart stopped in her chest and icy fingers seized her by the throat. She screamed out into the vast, narrow, black tunnel, "Where am I? What is this place? Take me *home!*"

He gathered her, silently, in both arms. With a speed and strength that should have terrified her - but of which, her senses reeling, she was heedless – he then brought her through one of the gaping, black maws in the tunnel wall to their right. Coming to her senses then, she did try to resist him, hit him, even bite him, but he had utterly pinned her arms in his and his confounding, white robe – bunching as it did around his hidden shoulders and neck – seemed to be utterly impervious to her wildly gnashing teeth.

He uttered something, a word, and at once a dazzling shaft of light poured down upon them from high above with a terrific crack and she ceased her struggles, falling silent, gaping. The tube of light in his hand winked out.

They were in a cavern very similar to the one in which she had awoken and the blue light coming from the roof fell upon and immersed a rock-hewn bed, perpendicular to the stone wall, which resembled very much the one in which she had lain. Her head reeling, she could do nothing to prevent him guiding her to this foreboding place and gently laying her down upon – or within – it, her head at the wall.

"You are in shock," said Brayton *(or is it Old Brayton or Illusion Brayton or just plain Nightmare Brayton),* soothingly, standing over her, his tall, thin, bent form eclipsing the light above, "Your emotional and psychological states may be unstable. Sudden rage and disorientation, perhaps even delusionary episodes may ensue. This is to be expected." He stood ram-rod straight then, peering down at her along his long, aqualine nose but the harshness of the light behind him prevented her from making out the expression of his eyes. "Even so I must try to lessen their impact upon your overall health status as much as possible."

Slowly, he knelt down at her elbow. Still woozy, she turned her head toward him, squinting.

"These futile struggles and episodes will not help us," he said to her, in a low voice, "Do you understand what I tell you?"

"Not help us," she repeated, mechanically, still squinting at him. His eyes were pools of shadow in the roof light. "Are you a prisoner, Brayton? Are *we* prisoners?"

"Shhh," he soothed. He rose, slowly, to his feet once more and looked down at her with his shadow-eyes. A tendril of fear slid slowly down her back. He leaned over and reached toward a shelf in the wall behind her head and withdrew a shining, white sheet from its shadows. This he gently lowered over her, cocking his head as he did so. "It is a name, a…..self-designation," he said.

She raised her arms and let the sheet cover her from arm-pit to toe. At once, she felt its heaviness and warmth even though it appeared to be thin, flimsy. Frowning up at him, she moved a hand to block out the light in order to see his face. "Excuse me," she said, licking her lips. Her mouth felt very dry. "Is what a name?"

"What you call me."

Again, she felt icy fingers trail along her spine in spite of the comforting warmth of the sheet. "It's your name, Brayton. Have you forgotten it?" she said, hoarsely.

"I have forgotten nothing," he said, blankly, swaying slightly over her, his eyes still shadows, "since I was born. At the Beginning."

Shocked, she saw him cock his head at her again and then turn away and lurch across the stone floor. *My God, what have they done to him? What has* IT *done to him?* She noticed that his peculiar shoes, or boots, or whatever they were, made no sound but a whisper as he stepped across the floor. He went and stood at the far wall and there seemed to freeze a moment. In the silence, she once again heard the sound of the distant waterfall beyond the open doorway, in the tunnel.

Slowly, keeping her eyes on his back, she sat up and swung her legs out over the edge of the bed. *Uh uh. Nobody's going to put me back in one of these things. Not even you, Shade-Hubby. Not while I still got my wits about me – for however much longer that might be.* Her head still spun and she felt the great weakness in her body, however. *Got to rest, though. And where would I even go?* Sitting upon the stone lip of the bed, she held a hand to her face.

Presently, Brayton lifted the darkened tube still clutched in his hand and she turned to watch him touch it to what looked a twin sitting upon a shelf of rock beside him. He uttered a word and it blazed into brilliant, blue life. In the same instant, at the four corners of the cavern, identical tubes alit as well.

She gasped in wonder.

"You will require," Brayton began, roughly, his back still to her, "nourishment in order to revive and strengthen." He spoke again – that word, that one word - and she heard a soft, cracking sound as a black opening appeared in the wall near him, perhaps three foot square, at floor level. She started, still wondering and still staring. It looked to her for all the world to be no more than a black pit of Gehenna, for all the bright illumination in the vast room failed utterly to penetrate it.

Brayton turned and, looking down at the small chasm himself a moment as if deciding that it was really there, advanced slowly toward it, squatting down carefully before its yawning mouth.

A white box was there and again she started in surprise, watching yet not comprehending.

"This," he grunted, grasping it and rising ponderously to his feet once more (reflexively, she stood up beside the bier-bed and half-stepped toward him to help him), "you will perhaps recall from past experience." He turned, holding the box out to her.

Her eyes seized upon it sitting there in his hands and her heart gave a lurch within her chest. A sheen of sweat stood out cold upon her forehead. She blinked. *Odd. It's just a box.*

He was holding it out to her, unmoving, his lined face impassive as he watched her. She moved towards him cautiously, eyes riveted upon the box in his hands. By the blue light all around her, she could see that it was not solid after all but was, rather, covered or draped in the same silky material that made up his boots and robes. She reached to take it. Her fingers brushed its white covering.....

(.....black, plasteel skin.....)
(.....shadowed recesses.....)

(.....and.....)

Her husband, aged, silent, head cocked, regarded her.

"It has a voice," she murmured, "this box."

She looked up at him, frowning, and slowly withdrew her fingers from the object in his hands. *Where did that come from? I don't get it. It's some kind of trap or trick.* Again, she was conscious of the dark place within her mind. "No, thanks," she said, in little more than a whisper, "I don't want it. Take it away."

A shadow flitted across Brayton's face. "I can give to you nourishment," he said, evenly, after a pause, "within this box. Each and every day. I can give to you clothing. I can give to you shelter. These things you require. It has been established." Her eyes widened. "If you do not desire the things which, by proof, it has been determined you need in order to survive," he shrugged, his dark eyes still blank, "then you will die."

Her mouth fell open. "My God," she whispered, "who are you? *What* are you?"

She struck him. Hard. All of the fear and anger and – she would later realize – even the guilt at having left him on the other side apart from her emptied themselves into the blow and it left a mark upon his withered face. For an instant, a fleeting moment, she thought she saw all of those same emotions upon *his* face, that it was a mirror of her own when the blow fell, but then they were gone, vanished as if she had only imagined them.

He staggered back, holding a long, thin hand to his face. He blinked and then the confounded, stoic expression returned to his eyes. "You have been banned from the place that was intended for you," he said, quietly, lowering his hand.

A soft hissing sound came abruptly to her ears.

"You will not be permitted to enter it again. Your behaviour, in future, however, may alter this decision."

The sound grew and began to fill the chamber. She glanced from him, still holding the queer box in his hand, to the open doorway to the tunnel and then all around them. Slowly, a dawning, terrifying comprehension came to her. Already she was beginning to gasp for air. "You bastard," she panted, "you've sold out to….." She fell to her knees, chest heaving. He regarded her coolly, without emotion. "You're with *her* now, aren't you?" She collapsed to the floor, head spinning, mouth open and gasping uselessly. "That thing," she whispered, dimly, "….. Shade-Sister….."

VII

"Mariss."

She mumbled, stirring faintly.

"Shh, don't make a sound."

"Wha-?" she muttered, "Sound?"

"Shhhh. Please."

She opened her eyes. A faint, blue glimmer surrounded her. Idly, she watched it glow upon the rocks directly above her head. "Blue," she whispered, "So blue."

"Down here."

She frowned.

"Near your head. At the floor."

She turned her head to the side but it swam so. It seemed to take an age for her eyes to lower toward the sound.

The Voice. The sound is the Voice. Not of Her - not of It. The Voice of the Box. The Voice of the Object.

"Object," she murmured, looking. She blinked and at last saw what she was looking at. A hole was situated in the bottom of the stone wall, right at her stone bed's very head. She had not noticed it when she had been brought here. Perhaps it had not existed then. Idly, she looked at it. Its opening was an empty, black maw. "Dark," she muttered, "Like all the rest".

"Quick," whispered a voice, from within the very throat of that darkness, "this might be the only chance. It's asleep. Can you move?"

Without warning, she began to cry. The tears were still slow in coming but they came. Her body, in that moment, felt as if it were made of lead, however, and there was no way that she could move it. Especially, not after she had heard the Voice after so long.

"Dammit!" said the voice, faintly, from within the hole, "She can't move. They've kept her alive but weakened, the bastards. I'll have to go out and get her."

Frowning, she heard other, cautioning sounds from within the blackness, other voices. She tried to assimilate them in her mind but couldn't. A deep fear seized her.

But then he came.

He was like a grey mist, for a worn, grey kerchief was tied around the lower half of his face and his eyes were obscured by a dark, red visor. His dark hair was long and unkempt, dishevelled, and she saw, idly, that it even reached to his shoulders. Dimly, she perceived that his broad arms were bare, that he wore a dark, tattered shirt with the sleeves rolled up. "Jock," she murmured, "always the jock."

Reflexively, he ducked and darted his gaze across the dimly-lit room, beyond her field of vision. "Don't try to speak," he hissed. "It's inactive right now."

Rising, he gently got his arms underneath her and, grunting, lifted her out of the stone bed within the warm, white sheet.

"I knew I'd find you," she whispered up at him.

Straining, he swivelled his body and lowered her toward the hole. "Take her, take her," he grated and she felt other hands grasp her and pull her into the maw. He followed after, soundlessly, and she saw him before her crouching in the aperture of the hole. He motioned, frantically yet silently, and she felt the others, dark shadows behind her, grasp her and pull her deeper into the blackness. She perceived that she was inside a small, narrow, tunnel-like tube through the rock, and thanked God, faintly, that she was not claustrophobic. Then Brayton – the real Brayton, her real, lost husband – was doing something and she tried to focus on what it was. He had extricated something from the pocket of a dark pair of trousers and she saw by the dim light of the cavern beyond that it was a tube identical to the one that his older doppel-ganger had held. Jutting his hand out of the hole, he levelled it toward one of its twins at the far end of the chamber and there was a sizzling pop.

Instinctively, she cried out, covering her eyes with her hand, as a blaze of blue shone in the tunnel. And then she realized *that it no longer had an opening behind Brayton.* He sat before her, leaning heavily against a rock wall. She gaped, even within the harsh light. Abruptly, however, the light decreased until it was only a faint, soft beacon in his hand.

"A magic trick," he said in a low voice, panting slightly, and pulling the kerchief down from his face and tucking it under his chin, "that we learned from -" he jerked his head behind him.

Before she could reply, he said to the others, "Give her some eyes."

Someone held out before her a dark visor and she slowly reached for it. She saw that her hand shook noticeably and saw that Brayton saw it too. He reached out and helped her to fix the device over her eyes.

"Ahh," she murmured, for, through the darkened lenses, she could see them there. There were three others crouching within the tunnel besides her and Brayton; she could see their bodies glowing yellow and orange and red whenever they moved.

"That," said Brayton, "is good, old-fashioned *human* magic. Infra-red."

"From the mission," she said, dazedly, "From the stores. What else - ?"

"We should go," interrupted one of the others, "It'll get a lock on us very soon thanks to that little magic trick."

The three others, she noticed, were two men and.....a woman. Mariss gasped. Twisting her head around, she whispered to the woman, who crouched directly behind her, "I know you. You are Larissa..... Larissa Ilsudova....."

The woman gave a shuddering sigh and reached to grasp Mariss's hand desperately in her own.

"Now," insisted the man who had spoken earlier. He had two deep, yellow lines across his face, parallel gashes, clearly visible in the infra-red and Mariss started again as another name thrust itself powerfully into her mind: *Leo.....Leonid Antonich Ilsudov.* A shiver went down her spine. *Husband and wife. So long ago they all departed, leaving us behind back on the Network. So long ago.*

Brayton was shaking his head. She saw that he was reaching into another pocket. "She needs energy first. And then we got to get her to her kit."

"My....." she said. *My kit. My equipment. My supplies.* "You've found my Scout," she croaked.

He shot her a glance but then thrust out toward her two small, white cubes in an open palm. "Here," he said, "Take them both. Quickly now."

She felt, rather than saw, Leo Ilsudov tense like a spring on her opposite side. She reached to take the emergency packets from her husband, each one, she knew, containing enough energy for several days. In a trembling hand, she brought them to her mouth and swallowed them down with difficulty. She grimaced. They tasted bitter, even foul, as if they were far beyond their expiry. He handed her a tube of water. "Brayton….." she began, huskily, "I….."

"Later, Mess," he said, gently, and a heart-felt giggle escaped her dry lips at that name, that silly moniker that he used to call her. It felt so good to hear it again. "All in good time. But right now you need to drink that up." He gestured at the tube in her hand. "It's from this place, wherever it is," he said, somewhat resignedly, waving his hand around them, "Better than any of the reclaimed water back home. And it seems to have extra efficacy for human metabolism."

Eagerly, she brought the tube to her lips and slowly sucked on it, feeling the blessed coolness of the water seep down her throat.

Then Ilsudov blurted in his thin, clipped, accented voice, "You had better be right about this precious wife of yours, Keppeler," ("Leo…..," gasped Larissa in a choked voice behind her, squeezing her hand.) "Not only have you endangered our position with this heroic rescue mission and with this magic stunt you've insisted on pulling but now you've taken a giant chunk out of our sustenance on this miserable rock, haven't you?" He bore his gaze on Mariss. "And all to save *her.*"

"Leo!" hissed his wife, "How dare you?"

Unmoved by her indignation, however, the Alpha executive officer stared at Mariss and, even though he wore the same, dark lenses that they all wore, she could both see and feel the blaze of hate in his eyes.

He never had any love for me. I remember that now. But I can't remember why. Maybe that was a blessing. "What does he mean," she murmured, turning her eyes to Brayton, "You better be right.....?"

But he cut her off, snarling, "If it was the other way around, Leo, I'd help you. Now let's move. The ante-chamber first."

Move they did, yet single-file, on elbows and knees, huffing in the narrow tube through the rock. Ilsudov, having been handed the soft, blue beacon of light by Brayton, led the way, followed by the other man whom she did not know or could not remember (she didn't know which it was but there was undoubtedly a difference due to that confounded empty space in her memory) and then Larissa immediately before her. Brayton brought up the rear, silently, a solid, welcome presence behind her.

Soon, however, in the narrow confines, Mariss felt that, claustrophobia or no, she would scream again and this time not stop. Her strange and wonderful blanket, she managed somehow to keep about her shoulders and its improbable warmth radiated through her body, helping her to keep from shivering, at the least, but she would not get truly warm, she knew, until she was wearing her coveralls once again. Indeed, it was the thought of possessing her full kit once more that was her real sustainer. It filled her with a keen anticipation much like she had felt when she had first received it from E.P.

More began to come back to her. Slowly and gradually, as she advanced, painfully, through the narrow shaft, other memories stirred within her mind. She nodded, grimly, to herself as she recalled that it was Idris, himself, who had given her her kit for the first time – for Beta.

He had been staunchly opposed to the mission, at first. *That* was a solid memory. Yet she had persisted and won over both the E.P. panel and then the Syndicate Board with what she had been told by one board member afterward was 'the inexorability of the eloquence of the sharpest mind of our generation." She scoffed - there in the small tunnel - as she recalled this. *Peculiar what one remembers.* She had not been sure of the assessment, herself, of course, but when the Director had finally called for the Mission across the NetLink and had told the Residents that once more an Arlen would lead them in their time of need, she remembered that she had been immensely grateful.

Yet all of that had come after Alpha had left, hadn't it? It had come well after she and Brayton had been modestly married in the Pacifica Module with the eerie, greenish glow of the vastness of Australia turning beneath them. *But about Leo…..I really don't remember. Something happened between us, though. I can feel it. Something lost –*

A tremor, deep below their plodding elbows and knees, shook her, made her teeth chatter.

"Faster!" hissed Brayton, from behind.

The ante-chamber was a low-roofed, broad scoop out of the rock. Nothing more. The five of them halted, spreading out, fan-like, before its end wall. Mariss, huffing slightly, but feeling stronger, glanced quickly around. The floor was of dust, dull grey in the blue light of Leo's beacon; dry, certainly, yet she noticed that it did not rise, cloyingly, into the air when they moved but remained wholly upon the floor. She moved her fingers through it. *Like the regolith of the moon beneath the boots of the first astronauts a century and a half ago. And of the Selena colonists after them. Before the War. I remember watching the boots shuffling through it on the vid-streams during the Evac when I was a girl. The* big *Evac just before the Launch. But there was no atmosphere there. And here we are breathing.*

"There," said Brayton, pointing. She saw that he had pulled the kerchief back up over his face. Following the direction of his extended finger, she made out two dark bundles lying in the dust against the far wall of the tiny chamber. She crawled toward them, the others parting for her. "What is this place anyway?" she murmured, "Did you make it?"

"No," said Brayton, behind her, "This one we found. I think it was the first, even." She turned to regard him over her shoulder and caught him shooting a quick glance at Ilsudov. "Back then, it was very hard. In those first days, we had to dig with our science implements and our bare hands if you can believe it. We literally carved out an existence."

She reached the bundles and, behind her, Ilsudov obligingly lifted the beacon and turned it so that she could make them out. She grasped the first in her hands, a ball of fabric, and turned it in trembling fingers. "Ah!" she cried, hoarsely, as a Syndicate mark briefly flashed in the light. She turned her head to look back at them as they crouched there, regarding her rigidly.

"Is it all there?" asked Brayton, his voice taut, "Is it all intact? Everything?"

She felt for and riffled through the pockets. Supplements. A tiny light. Even the digital micro-labe, which Idris had insisted on giving her, so that she could take bearings on the Other Side. She gave a snicker and pulled it out, holding it in her palm in Ilsudov's light. She saw them all strain forward, staring at it. It had not been a part of the Alpha crew's kit, she recalled. The *Alpha* had been equipped with all of the instrumentation that the Syndicate could provide, far beyond her own, later, more meagrely outfitted scout-ship. She jiggled the tiny device in her hand. "Yeah," she said, amazed, "it's all here – *so far.* I don't believe it. Nothing lost..... or taken." She looked up at them. "How long - ?"

Brayton let out his breath, slowly, as if he had been holding it in for days. "All in good time, Mess," he said, visibly relaxing before her eyes, "Believe it or not, this was absolutely key whether or not It/They had taken anything of yours. We've watched these bundles desperately since finding them." She inclined her head, inquiringly, but he held up a hand.

"More, later," he said. He looked over at Ilsudov once more and Mariss saw that the Russian and his wife had now drawn together and that Larissa briefly laid her head on his shoulder. "There is a lot that has happened to us," said Brayton,"....before *and* after you came."

"Of course," Mariss murmured, regarding them all. She slipped the tiny device back into a pocket and then held up her coveralls before her for a brief moment in the soft, beacon light. She saw her name beneath the brand on the left chest. "I am," she breathed, "Dr. Mariss Arlen Keppeler after all. My life was not a dream - or an illusion. But now I must find it again."

There was a brief silence and then Ilsudov lowered the tube of light in his hand. She let the white sheet she had wrapped about her shoulders fall to the dust and half-rising within the small chamber – as much as the low ceiling would allow her – began to step into her coveralls. Oh, how she wished for a hot shower, even a tepid one, at that moment but she knew it might be a long, long time before she could enjoy such luxuries.

Then even though she could not see him, a sharp awareness of Ilsudov's eyes upon her as she stepped into her working clothes came over her. She felt them crawl over her body. Shuddering, she zipped up her old uniform tightly to her chin as quickly as she could.

He doesn't love Larissa. He never did.

The thought, like so many lately, crashed through into her consciousness from that dark place in her mind like a bull through a china shop window. She felt her insides churn.

A faint smell of smoke came to her nostrils in the cool air. She frowned. *The coveralls?* She raised an arm to her nose, sniffing. *No. Not smoke. Ozone.* She thought no more of it. Then, with a final adjustment, a final tug, she was a uniformed officer of Mission Beta One again. She took in a deep breath in the cool, stale air of the rock chamber and turned to face the others.

Brayton was regarding her silently, his dark lenses opaque, Larissa and the other man gaping up at her.

Involuntarily, her eyes slid to Ilsudov

(.....black, dead eyes.....)
(.....clammy fingers.....)
(.....no air.....)

and then back to Brayton, her brow slick and her chest heaving.

"Whoa, are you all right?" said Brayton, alarmed. He half-rose and moved toward her.

"I'm.....I'm fine," she murmured, frowning, "Just queasy. I think my body just needs to get used to this real nutrition after so long."

He visibly relaxed again. "Right," he said, "Of course. You'll need to take it slow, okay?"

She nodded.

"And, by the way, your boots are there behind you."

Crouching in her coveralls, she turned and reached for them. Sitting in the chamber-dust, she carefully put them on while the others silently watched and then she reached for the second bundle that lay in the dust of the chamber floor.

This one was much heavier and bulkier, as she knew it would be. They had come far in the advancement of suit technology in the years before the War, her father had told her long ago. Manufacturing and development had been transferred to the labs at Selena, honing the environmental specs of new and better suits beautifully in the lunar milieu. There was the desire to return to Mars and re-claim *Aries*, the sprawling, inter-connected, multi-domed habitat. It had been left high and dry by the *Proteus* disaster, when the latest crafts had all been destroyed in a horrible chain-reaction explosion almost sixty years ago. There was the grand plan to reach it again, revive and expand it, make it a viable option once again for humanity's growing needs, its rapidly dwindling resources on Earth. The better suits would do that, her father had said. *Would have done that. If the failing resources after Proteus hadn't touched off the frenzied struggles between Peoples, the gashing open of old, old wounds in the hearts of archaic nations…..If the War hadn't swept through the middle of a burgeoning spring day like a giant scythe of wintry Death. If the Collective had never been.*

If, if, if.

She held her own space-suit up before her in the soft, blue light of Leo's raised beacon. Its rigid bulkiness and cumbersome appearance testified to the tragedy that had befallen them all in the last two generations – had befallen her entire, brilliant, yet mad, vain-glorious race.

"It looks good," she said, absently, "No visible damage."

"Then come on," said Brayton, in reply, "we've been crawling enough. Time to take you home." He grinned at her before setting the kerchief back up over his face.

VIII

Home was a cavern with no roof-light.
It was a chamber like all the others, as far as Mariss could tell, except its floor was of dust and not rock and it had no crack in its ceiling. The only illumination came from six evenly-spaced tubes strewn about its floor like luminescent, blue candles. A few huddled shadows were grouped around them and she spied what appeared to be a few, squat machines against the walls.

They were all doffing their visors now and so Mariss did the same, absently hooking it into a pocket of her coveralls.

"We stole the lights from *It…..Them…..Whoever,*" said Brayton, pulling down the kerchief from his mouth, "They seem to be emplaced within each and every chamber inside the Mother – what we call this mountain. De-activated. We learned how to activate them. We've tried to explore all of the cha-"

She pointed at his kerchief. "Why do you wear that?"

He stared at her, confused, for a moment. "Oh," he said, "this." He tugged at the kerchief tied round his neck. He shrugged and looked around the chamber. "None of the others seem to have this problem, but if I don't wear it regularly, I get this dry hitch and a terrible cough...."

"It is true," said Ilsudov, carefully enunciating each English word, and leading his wife by the hand so that they stood with her and Brayton. Mariss's eyes wandered to the double gash on the side of his face and an involuntary shudder went through her. "He was 'laid up' I believe you American Sectors say, for many, many hours after we first settled in here."

"And off and on over the years since," said Brayton. He let his words sink in.

Mariss looked at him and at Leo and Larissa and then around the chamber at each of the shadows huddled around the softly gleaming, blue tubes. *Years. And they like refugees. All of them here. Alien refugees.* She gulped, dryly, heart quickening. Was this not what she had suspected deep down? What she had feared? "How long - ?" she managed, in a hoarse voice.

."I think it's time to tell you the story. The story of *Alpha,*" said her husband, quietly, "And that's going to include some of the gripping tale of *Beta* as well. Then we are going to need to show you something – a few 'somethings,' actually. But not before you hear what we have to say." Again, he looked over at the Ilsudovs.

"Yes, and then perhaps you will answer a question for *us,*" put in Leo, turning his dark gaze upon her, the gashes at the side of his face quivering, "You are the only person who can answer it. We all agree about this. But your husband here -" he glanced back at Brayton a moment" - he seems to believe something else, something more; that you are the only person who can rescue us, who can bring us somewhere *different.*" He smiled, wryly. "And about *this,* there is a little *less* agreement."

John Naishen turned the tiny device in his hand. "And so it could plot our co-ordinates on a stellar map?" he asked her. He held it up before his eye.

"Yes," she said, "but first I would need more data." She remembered him as little more than a fresh-faced youth from the Euro Sector when he had launched forth with the others from the Network. Now his be-whiskered, matured face bespoke the passage of time more eloquently than her husband's quiet words had. It had filled her with an irrational terror but she would not reveal that to them. She could not.

They were seven all told, not including her, even though they said they were the same number they were when they had departed. One was lost, she had already heard, and two were not there at that moment. The math didn't make sense to her. Yet. John handed the device back to her and she slid it back into the breast-pocket of her coveralls. She said, "I would need to stand out on the surface, outside the Mountain, er, the Mother. You understand? I would need to use it as an inclinometer against that wonderful, blue sun, and check our latitude." She laughed. "I could make sure when it was the proper time for tea."

A whisp of a smile touched his weary face.

"It could also be used to calculate distances between points, between celestial objects and, based upon our own known co-ordinates here on this planet or moon, could plot our position on stored, stellar maps, yes."

The young man leaned forward from the circle in which they all sat upon plastic and metal containers. Two of the blue, tube lanterns, as she liked to think of them, had been brought to sit near them, affording them enough good light to see one another clearly. She could see that he was animated by a growing, though wary, enthusiasm and that he was not the only one. "So it might be able to figure out *which* galaxy we are in?"

She nodded. "Based upon existing archival data, of course. Now, my scout-ship was also equipped with your electronic and thermal signatures. If you were within tracking or sensing distance, if you had reason to fire your thrusters to change attitude or trajectory or velocity, I would have been able to *see* your plasma foot-prints, so to speak, and hopefully contact you, point you the way back."

"Back through the Portal?" he said. She saw him tremble and fire a quick, eager glance at Brayton and Leo Ilsudov who sat opposite her in the circle. Brayton was also leaning forward, his elbows on his knees and his fingers steepled against his mouth. She saw Leo sitting beside him, leaning back, arms crossed. They both had grim, though thoughtful, expressions on their faces.

"That's wonderful," said Brayton, wearily, after a while, "except the location of the Doorway is already known. Or.....thereabouts. We already know approximately where it is." Ilsudov grunted in agreement. "And it's not *out* there," Brayton went on, sitting up straight and waving his arm over his head toward the roof of the cavern. "Not in space, not in orbit..... we don't need our faithful, old ship to reach it. Or even yours."

Mariss stared at him, wide-eyed. "Where is it then?"

He brought his arm down and pointed at the grey, dust-covered ground. "It's here. In the Mother. *Somewhere.*"

Ilsudov stirred. "You see, Dr. Keppeler," he said, slowly and carefully, "when *Alpha* passed *beyond*, we found ourselves here." He spread out his arms and turned looking all around them. "That is the story, that is the.....mysterious tale that we have for you. There was no great....*labyrinth,* yes,.....of beckoning Gateways, no super network of dimensional Spaces from which we could pick and choose our new terrestrial paradise as if we were at a - how do you say? - 'buffet'." His eyes glowed malevolently at her. "Such as you and all of the rest of our top minds -" (Mariss saw his lip curl ever so slightly at this) "back on the Network posited in your glossy papers. No. We did not travel through space, we did not consult our on-board computer for....." he paused, scratching his head, "*stellar.....co-ordinates*. Or ask fascinating, tiny, little devices such as the one in your little pocket there for directions." He shrugged. "I found myself walking, stumbling through the dust, through the dark....."

"He found me," put in Brayton, jerking his head toward the opening of the cavern behind Mariss, "Out there. Slumped by the water-fall. Coughing my lungs out but breathing. Barely. And the others?" He tapped the side of his head. "In here. Calling. Their voices....." He shuddered.

Mariss swallowed, dryly, again, her head feeling light.

Ilsudov leant forward. "Personally, I believe now that *It* –" he glanced up at the ceiling of grey rock "– our Host, helped us to find one another in the dark. Telepathically. And It allowed us to find and activate the beacons. And to wander freely through *most* of these chambers. As far as the oxygen extends."

Mariss gasped. "But *why?*" she blurted, "What does it *want*? Do you still not know what it is?"

"It's God in here," cried John Naishen, standing, his shrill voice echoing sharply off the walls and ceiling, "Haven't you figured that out yet? It's trapped us all in here like so many rats in a maze, dangling things before our eyes, things we want, things we'd give anything for, and then yanking them away again. It gets Its thrills from it. We are Its pets. It's created that old, twisted version of Captain Keppeler for *you* because It wants to torture you with it!"

"John." Brayton was reaching a hand toward him but the youth was not finished. His grey eyes were bleak with despair and his mouth trembled. "That's why Dallicet left," he moaned, "Why she went outside. It tricked her into thinking someone had landed and was trying to communicate with us. It put voices into her head to lure her out there! I know It did. And all because It could!"

Mariss whistled, softly. *Dallicet. Dallicet Ollenas. Communications. My God, I remember them all now. Flooding back into my head. One by one.*

Brayton stood up. "John," he said, holding up a hand toward him, "Don't do this to yourself."

John turned his back and, shaking uncontrollably, lurched off toward the far wall.

Brayton let out a long sigh and he seemed to deflate before her eyes. "Mariss," he said, then, and he beckoned to her. She got up and most of the *Alpha* crew in the rough circle rose with her.

He led her to one of the strange-looking machines huddled against the wall of the cavern. She stood over it as he reached out and tapped it with his fingers.

"The *Alpha* was gone the instant we appeared here," he said in a low voice. "We've never found it…..*physically*. But we've since found these."

She looked down at the machine before her more closely in the blue light. Its sides were stripped away, showing motherboards and circuitry within its bowels and its edges looked as if they had been sawn, cut, *ripped away*. Dials, gauges stood out upon its surface. It struck her after a moment's bewilderment. "This is…..part of the engine sub-systems….." she murmured, lost.

Brayton nodded. "Very good, Mess. You still have some of that rapier mind of yours left after that *thing* finished with it. That's what I'm counting on. And you're right, this is part of the containment system for the nuclear core."

She gasped, her hand over her mouth. "Then where is the - ?"

He shook his head. "Gone," he whispered, "No trace of it has ever been found. We don't have any sensory equipment, very little equipment of any kind actually, and so we can't search it out. We've got nothing to go on." He moved to another shape against the wall and she saw right away that it was another ripped out section of the *Alpha'* s drive level. She was beginning to feel nauseous. "This one was the temperature and containment integrity monitor," he said, "It had to dismantle both of these to get to…..it. We found each of these in adjoining chambers. Just sitting on the ground. We couldn't figure it at first but, of course, eventually we put two and two….."

"It was the power," Mariss murmured, "Wasn't it? It wanted the power. Maybe It…..can sense it or feel it. Maybe It *eats* power the way we eat food." She felt sick.

Turning, tottering, then, she took in, one by one, all of the lanterns, the tubes, the lights of blue strewn about the chamber and the paltry number of former *Alpha* crew-members who had huddled round them hastily moved out of her way.

"Zzzz…..ZEN-ya!" she shouted.

The tube lights, for an instant, blazed blindingly and it was as if the alien, blue sun had peeked in at them through the doorway of the cavern. Mariss felt heat, like a fire, for a moment upon her skin and there came the sharp, acrid tang of ozone on the air.

She was blind.

Or rather *blinded.* She heard the cries of the others echoing within the chamber of rock around her but could not make anything out.

"Who said that?" screamed a voice and it was the voice of Leo Ilsudov, rising above the commotion.

"It was me," she croaked, shaken, "I didn't mean to -"

And then a massive tremor shook the cavern and she felt herself pitched to the dust floor on her face. This one lasted a full ten seconds easily although it seemed like it would go on and on and not stop until the Mountain itself had collapsed in on them. Dust was in her mouth and up her nostrils and everywhere else it could possibly enter. She coughed, violently though dryly. They were all coughing and gasping and she could feel the dust caking her skin.

Suddenly, there came a *whoosh* - Mariss felt it soft upon her cheek – and she looked up and found she could see again. Dimly, her coughing subsiding, she perceived that a black opening had appeared in the wall opposite her, a large, upright doorway with bright, flickering, blue light issuing from it into the darkened cavern. She realized, then, that all of the tubes in the large room had gone out. Startled, she noticed that a woman was silhouetted in the newly gaping hole.

"Larissa!" called the woman, urgently, in a dry, rasping voice, "Where are you? Come quick!"

Wahlia Deepa......Geologist.

"Here," gasped Larissa Ilsudova, struggling to her feet and covered in dust, "I am here. Is she okay? Is she hurt?"

"It's her foot," choked Wahlia. "It's caught."

"Ah!" exclaimed Larissa, clutching her husband's arm. Leo was helping her to her feet and together they began to stumble toward the opening.

Brayton was bending down toward her. "You okay?" he gasped. He had raised the cloth back up over his face and dust coated his forehead. He reached out and grasped her arm, helping her to her feet. She stood, unsteadily, absently brushing off her cover-alls. "Come on," he said, pulling her by the arm toward the opening, "we were going to show her to you after. Hopefully she'll be all right."

Frowning, her free hand held up to her face, Mariss followed Brayton through the dust and into the newly-gaping hole.

This room, she took in in a moment, was of rock alone. Indeed, there was no dust at all except that which they brought with them from the main chamber, tracking it on the rock floor, billowing it into the damper, chiller air in here. To her nostrils, there came a different tang. The air was different.
They were all shouting around her frantically, "….. Get the diggers!.....Get some levers down there. Maybe we can lever it out…..Is it broken?....Is she still conscious?"
"Mama! Papa!" screamed a high, shrill, child-like voice, *"Pomogite! Bol'no!"*

She froze, the blood turning to ice within her veins. Shaking, like a sickness, seized her.

Brayton went ahead. There were bodies passing to and fro around her, eclipsing the blue light in the room. Her arm still up before her face even though there was no more dust to ward off, she squinted everywhere, straining to see. The lit tubes in here seemed to be everywhere, shining like azure candles on the stone floor, not snuffed out, not dead.
At last, the bodies parted and her feverish glance fell upon a little figure leaning perilously against, and clutching desperately to, two of the *Alpha* crew members. Her heart gave a lurch when she saw that they were Leo and Larissa Ilsudov.

"Dorogoy, dorogoy," soothed the mother.

Mariss shook her head and stepped back.

The child was facing away from her, wearing a short, party dress, and long, black hair tied and done up in ringlets upon its back.

Mariss took another step backward, her mind screaming at her. It was wrong, illogical, it did not follow. Yet, evidently, she was the only one to see it.

John and Brayton and the others were all chinking at the stone floor with crude implements while Leo and Larissa stood clutching the child, faces pale. *"Bol'no!"* it wailed, *"Bol'no."* Mariss's frantic eyes swivelled to the floor and she saw for the first time that it had opened up, a jagged gash in the rock, and had swallowed the child's right leg up to the knee.

"What are you *doing?*" she shrieked, "Leave It alone. Just leave It there! It's trapped. It can't hurt us."

They paid her no heed but continued to chip and chink. Fragments of rock littered the floor and, for long while, the improbable, mysterious child's whimpering was the only other sound.

At last, they pulled free the tiny leg. Gently, Leo and Larissa eased it out of the fissure in the floor and Larissa enfolded the child in her arms, sobbing with joy and relief. "If anything had happened to you," whispered the mother, in English, "If anything had happened to you….."

"No!" shouted Mariss, shaking her head, and the others, who had been murmuring in sympathy, fell silent, turning toward her. "It's another illusion. It's not logical. *Think* about it."

Leo Ilsudov stood, open-mouthed, staring at her. Then she saw his black eyes glitter with rage. Larissa slowly turned toward her, still clutching the child, her face wet. Her bleary, blue eyes registered disbelief.

"John," said Mariss, urgently appealing to the youth standing beside Ilsudov. He stood in stunned silence, a digging implement hanging limply in his right hand. "Is this not something that *It* would do? Create an illusion to entrap us in? Fiddle with our heads?"

"But," said the young European, hesitantly, and looking at her bewilderedly, "this is not…..It can't control the earthquakes or make fissures in the rock floor….."

"It can make cracks in the ceiling," she pointed out.

"Only the *word* can do that," said Ilsudov, testily, "I've seen it happen, I've heard it spoken. But never by telepathy, never out loud as a disembodied voice. Only by a real, live manifestation of *It* - only by an avatar."

Mariss shuddered and stared, helplessly, fearfully, at the small child, still sniffling, still nestled in Larissa's arms, its head upon its mother's far shoulder.

Dawning comprehension entered into Ilsudov's black eyes.

"Ah," he said, bitingly, "and my daughter is one of them, yes? She is a…..*manifestation?*"

An utter silence followed.

Then Ilsudov spat violently on the ground and stepped forward, lips twisting with rage. His black eyes blazed at her. Brayton stepped out, protectively, from the ranks of crew-members gathered around them, interposing himself between them.

"I would sooner believe that the eminent Dr. Mariss Arlen Keppeler," Ilsudov shouted, black eyes boring into hers, "standing so exalted here before us, is the manifestation. *She* is the creature. She uses the word!"

For a moment, no-one spoke, no-one moved.

Brayton raised a hand toward him. "Leo," he said, quietly, "let's not get paranoid here. Let it go. She didn't mean to offend you. Or your family. She doesn't know. She doesn't know how much *time* we've been trapped here. Okay? She doesn't *know.*"

Mariss's head reeled and she stared at the little figure with the ringlets and the party dress as if her eyes would pop from their sockets. Her throat worked but no sounds came.

"Mariss? *Mariss!*"

She jerked her head up. Brayton was holding out toward her a beseeching hand, and in his brown eyes she saw a desperate, silent appeal.

"Just now, I told you we had some things to show you but *not* before you had heard what we had to say. Do you remember that?"

She jerked her head again.

"And that was because," he went on, "you would not be ready for it. You would not be prepared." He took in a deep breath and glanced at the Ilsudovs – all three of them. "Today – as near as we can tell – is Lara's fifth birthday. *That* is how long we have been trapped here. Do you understand? At least that long." He nodded at Larissa, still kneeling and holding her daughter. "Her mother made her a dress. Painstakingly. With her own hands and modified needles and fabric It took her months. Okay? Larissa had become pregnant - again as near as we could tell – a few months after we came here. By her husband, of course." A whisp of a smile came to his thin, drawn face.

Mariss felt her heart straining within her coveralls. For a long time, she was silent. "I.....accept the time of years," she said, finally. Her eyes were still riveted upon the child. ".....For you. All of you." She darted her gaze to all of the faces around her. "I believe what you say. Only -" she turned, beseechingly, to the Ilsudovs, a hand raised toward them, and swallowed with difficulty – "I just need to see its face. You don't understand why. But I need to see its eyes."

Ilsudov cursed under his breath in Russian but his wife stirred. "No," she said, "it is all right." She spoke to the child in a low voice and Mariss saw it nod its head. Larissa then slowly turned the tiny figure toward Mariss by its small shoulders but the child held its head down, black hair covering its face.

"Pokazat,'" said the mother, softly, *"milaya dama vashego krasivoye litso."*

Slowly, the child raised its head and Mariss's heart hammered within her body as if from far, far away - as if it were buried within another rock chamber deep inside the Mother. *It's trying to scare me, unhinge my mind. I know it is.*

"Krasivoye litso," cooed Larissa, gently sweeping the long hair from the face, "Pretty face."

Mariss's helpless gaze fell upon small, black, opaque eyes, impenetrable, inscrutable. But not in-human. *Chillingly like her father's, though, and they're ALMOST in-human.* She shuddered.

Then the girl turned and clutched at her mother, hiding her face once more.

"There!" said Ilsudov, indignant, "Are you satisfied?"

"Mariss," said Brayton, coming over and grasping her by the right fore-arm. She blinked, dumbly, after the girl as he slowly guided her from the lit chamber. "I think it's time, high time, to show you one last thing….."

IX

She wasn't sure when she had quite returned her full attention to her surroundings, to the long, narrow, echoing tunnel stretching out before her once more. Her head had been filled with images of Solea long gone, stirring up emotions still raw and intense. Her sister's face, her face so alive and beautiful, just as she remembered it, so full of the vitality of life. And then the hollow shell that it had become just before the end after the radiation had worked its merciless cruelty.

Crying out, she stumbled to her knees. Stones and pebbles stabbed painfully into her flesh but she felt them only distantly. The nausea that she had felt in the lit chamber spiked and she brought her hand to her stomach, doubling over.

Brayton's hand tightened upon her fore-arm and she gave a violent start. He had knelt down beside her. "I can't," she croaked to him, "Just give me a bit."

His hand remained on her arm but she felt it ease its grip. She noticed, abruptly, with a sudden, impotent rage, that he was holding one of the confounded, ever-present, blue, lit tubes in his other hand. Would they ever escape this place? Maybe it *was* hell.

After a moment, the nausea passed, at least the sharpness of it, and she staggered back to her feet, light-headed. Brayton rose and stepped back as she did so.

The sound of falling water came to her ears. Far away.

"The waterfall," she whispered, hopefully, turning to him, "We're going back to the waterfall."

He had pulled the kerchief back up over his face and she saw only his tired, blue eyes, grey in the light of his beacon. "No," he said, firmly, and, reaching out and grasping her arm, he began to lead her along the tunnel once more. Mechanically, she moved with him. *Deeper? Or toward the surface, toward the fall, even if not to it?* Her head spun unsettlingly.

"It's something else," he said, in a low voice, after a while. "Nearby. Almost like a shrine." He gave a dull snicker. "Maybe one day it will be."

Confused, she remained silent.

He grunted. "In here." He had stopped, holding the tube before them, revealing the black maw of a chamber that led off from the tunnel. There was no light within it. She could feel cooler air brush against her cheek. She looked at him and shivered.

"It's déjà vu," she said, quietly, "I've been here before. Walking through this tunnel. With you. Only not you."

He shook his head. "Not in this place," he said through his kerchief. "And in here you won't be held against your will, I can promise you that. In fact, in here you'll very likely be the happiest you've been since you came here. Six months, to be exact." He regarded her with those weary, though somehow calm, eyes. "That's when we first discovered this place and knew you were here. Somewhere." He shook his head, dolefully, then looked up sharply toward the opening. "And now it will all be worth it. Bringing you here at last. You might just make all of the rest of us the happiest we've been in a long while too. And that's five years. Maybe six. We just can't tell." He returned his solemn gaze to her. "Trust me on this."

She frowned at him and wrapped her arms about herself, still shivering, but then slowly and cautiously stepped forward into the darkened room. "What is it?" she asked. "It's too dark to see anything."

Yet that was not entirely true. She halted and waited as her eyes adjusted themselves to the dark and discerned a dim glow emanating from the rear wall of the chamber.

"Ahead," Brayton whispered in her ear. He had followed her, swiftly and silently as a shadow, and she jumped. She could sense his voice electric with a barely-contained emotion now.

She stood still within the dark room of stone, however, the chill air trembling around her, and made no move to go farther. "What is it?" she repeated in a hushed voice, her skin crawling with goose-prickles, "What's back there?"

"You must go," he said, quietly, "Marisseena."

She shot him a quick glance in the dimness – his tube-light had gone out - but his attention, indeed every fibre of his being, was now straining toward the far opening in the rock wall from whence shone dully a blue light. She turned back to it. And stepped toward it.

Mariss Keppeler blinked in amazement up at the side wall of the hidden chamber, momentarily blinded to everything else. Its entire surface, even the rock itself, was suffused with a softly gleaming, wavering, blue light. Indeed, it seemed to flow through the rock like myriad rippling, undulating veins. *Like a living thing.* Fascinated, she reached a hand toward it.

"No," said Brayton in a hushed, almost choked voice behind her, "You must not touch the rock. In this place it is.....sacred."

A sudden hot feeling surged through her as he said this and she jerked her hand away from the wall. In that same moment, the object upon which the ethereal light fell finally caught her attention and she whirled toward it.

It sat bathed in the light upon a raised, grey platform of rock in the middle of the chamber, dominating it as a showpiece, a prized display at a museum.

"My scout-ship," she whispered.

It squatted on its four stubby pads, like a large, black fly, its bulbous cockpit tilted slightly upward, facing toward the phosphorescent rock wall. It was impossibly small. "Did I really come in that?" she asked aloud and her hushed voice whispered amongst the rock walls. Shaking, she stepped forward, jerkily, and reaching up on tip-toe, laid a hand upon its smooth, plasteel underside.

She could remember nothing.

And wasn't that strange? The Creature had wiped her memory of all traces of the tiny craft. It must have. She had no recollection of piloting it, of flying it, no memory even of it ever having been physically *real!*

Shaking her head in consternation, murmuring to herself, she realized that the last solid recollection she had of it was as a digital rendering upon Newton Idris's desk console! "Yes," she whispered into the chamber. The sound of her voice hissed amongst the rock. "Exactly. It was going to be for one person, one person alone, someone not afraid to go – and perhaps never return." She swallowed as she remembered the exchange in the Director's office what seemed an age ago. *And would I go? That was what he asked me. Was that what I really wanted?*

"I didn't catch that," said Brayton, anxiously, behind her. She gave a start and turned to see him standing within the doorway to the inner room, his kerchief pulled down under his chin, his body leaning eagerly forward over the threshold, yet rooted outside of it, his un-lit blue tube hanging limply in his hand. She cleared her throat. "No memory," she said, huskily, to him before returning her gaze to the ship. "I have no memory of it at all."

Her fingers stretched out and brushed the rough skin of the space-craft once more. Then they stopped dead. This time it was unmistakeable.

Heat-scoring.

A chill went through her.

No sudden appearance in this place for me. Not if I came in this. This ship has penetrated and passed through atmosphere.

She glanced back at her husband over her shoulder. He was still tense, still leaning, still straining toward the ship, oblivious of her.

There is a lie somewhere.

"What is it?" he called, hoarsely, not looking at her, "Have you found any damage?" All but swaying on his feet, he kept turning his gaze this way and that around her as if trying to examine the small ship from all angles at once. But from a distance. She caught an almost keen terror in his eyes. "Can you still get inside?"

She turned back to the tiny, one-man craft, staring up at it, withdrawing her hand. *Inside? How do I do that?* A rising panic began to well up within her. Her brain, her mind, held nothing, it could not remember, could not remember a damned *thing*.....

.....and yet, automatically, almost involuntarily, she went aside and began to clamber up the pedestal of rock, keeping her eyes firmly fastened upon the tiny ship perched atop it. Again, she stretched out her hands towards its dark, plasteel skin and this time she watched in amazement as they slid slowly, gently, along its side of their own accord as if they were strange creatures beyond her control. They stroked the ship's skin as if they were caressing a lover and soon her fingertips found a hidden line, a crease within the side of the fuselage, and began to trace an intricate geometric pattern along it.

There was a sharp hiss and she stepped back, startled, almost plummeting from the plinth upon which she stood.

A hatch appeared within the side of the scoutship, sliding down to her feet.

"Aaah," she heard Brayton sigh behind her, "Sensory tactile input. Bio-metric data. We had guessed." Casting a backward glance at him again, she saw that his eyes were now fastened upon *her* with a feverish glow. "You see now how it has waited for you, Mariss, My Love, and how it has defied us for six months," he breathed. "And even the Creature Itself. I know it has. It will listen only to you. It will obey only you. Now you must see if it is still operable." He licked his lips.

Slowly, heart thudding, she turned back to the scout-ship. *Beta-One. It's called Beta-One.* Her nostrils flared as she faced the open hatch. Ozone. The gas seemed to be entwining long, thin arms through the air around her from the inside of the tiny ship. She stepped forward toward the opening and slowly leant inside.

(.....bright, blue flashes.....)
(.....hands convulsing on palm-grips.....)
(.....crushed chest.....)
(.....screams.....)

Gasping, thrusting her arms out to her sides and feeling the sides of the hatch, she paused a moment. Every hair on her body was on end and her mind began to rush with tattered, whirling images - but phantoms only, nothing tangible. She breathed for a long while. Just breathed. Then, at last, when she felt she could continue, she began to mount the small, narrow steps that led up into the cockpit.

"Are you all right?" she heard her husband call after her from far away. She did not respond.

A large, ergonomic, foam chair sat within the cockpit, surrounded by consoles. She surveyed it a moment, studying, analyzing, trying to recall. But nothing further came. The rushing images within her mind were already dissipating. *It's what It's done to me. It's fucked up my head too much.* Carefully, with a ragged groan, she lowered herself into the chair. Her body sank deep down within it. *I would be in my suit. The proportions would fit if I were in my suit.* Her stomach heaved dangerously and she laid her head back against the seat. She could feel the memory foam begin to enfold her, creating a mold of her body. She closed her eyes, hands pressed down hard over her stomach. And waited.

Now what?

"Mariss! What's happening? Are you okay?" From far away.

A deep, deep rumbling. From far beneath her, far beneath the ship.

Her eyes snapped open. Surprising herself, she croaked, *"Beta-One.* Initialize Emergency Protocol Over-ride."

There came a soft chime within the cock-pit and she gave a start within the chair even as she knew it would sound. Her heart beat a tattoo in her ears.

"Ident, please," said a soft, electronic, female voice. She jerked her head, glancing quickly around. Multiple, recessed speakers within the consoles materialized before her eyes.

"Ident," she said more clearly and her voice began to grow in clarity and in force, the words coming from a place she knew not where, "Commander Doctor Mariss Arlen Keppeler. Commission Date: Two-One-Two-Niner-One-Zero-Two-Five."

There was a pause. Her heart strained within her coveralls and a sheen of perspiration stood out on her face and hands.

"Ident and Commission Date confirmed," said *Beta-One,* at last, *"Voice harmonics recognized. Welcome, Commander. Emergency Protocol Over-ride initialization held in abeyance pending Command Authorization."*

She let out a small gasp and sat uncertainly within the huge chair. The inspiration she had had, the hidden knowledge coming to the fore when she had had desperate need of it seemed to ebb. *Oh, God, help me…..*

"Good luck, Commander," whispered Newton Idris in her ear, causing her to start violently, *"Your father took the small step. Now you will take the leap."*

Eyes bulging, hyper-ventilating, her hands felt for the grips of the chair and clenched them tight. The Network Director was not in the cockpit. This was an absolute fact. He was within her mind.
Only it was not him.
"Get out of my head," she croaked.

What does it mean: You will take the leap? I don't understand. Why did he say that to you?

"Get *out!*"

Does it concern final loss of power? I know about that.

She cried out within the chair, jaw clenching. *"Beta-One,"* she groaned through gritted teeth. She was keeping It away (**Why don't you tell me?**) keeping It desperately away but she could not do so for long. This too was an absolute fact. Dimly, through the fury inside her head, she heard the chime sound again.

"Emergency Protocol Over-ride," she rasped, "Command Authorization......" She winced, gritting her teeth so that she thought they might grind to dust within her mouth. ".....Alpha.....Sierra.....Four......Zero......Zero."

There came a double chime now and then another pause.

Finally.....

"Command Authorization acknowledged," the ship said, quietly, *"There will be no further abeyance of Routine Commands."* A recessed panel began to glow in the console directly before her. It slid open before her wildly-staring eyes.

Automatically, without thought or command, for indeed it was all she could do now to keep herself together, her right hand lashed out of its own accord and slid within the open panel, her fingers splayed. She winced as a bright, red laser scanned her palm and fingers.

At once, electronic panels throughout the cockpit began to glow. A myriad array of tiny lights flickered into being, most a deep green, some a warning amber, a few a bright red. A hum, low and intense, arose from the innards of the tiny ship beneath her which she felt more than heard. It seemed to tremble through her great, contoured chair.

The Creature vanished from her mind. In the same instant that the ship came to life, she felt it release its grip upon her thoughts and flee.

She leant back against the head-rest again, sighing in relief - so rigid had she become – and let the hum and the trembling immerse her.

"Emergency Protocol Over-ride Initialization commencing," said *Beta-One*, softly, through the vibrations of the ship, *"Exiting Hibernation Mode and terminating Lock-Out Status."*

She felt a lump in her throat. "Go with All Systems Check," she gasped. She realized that there were tears in her eyes.

"Acknowledging Go for All Systems Check. All grids coming on-line. Monitoring Power Source."

She began to laugh, sitting there, enfolded within the contours of her enormous chair, and then to cry, her shoulders shaking.

"Now take me home," she sobbed. "Just take me home."

X

"Can you see it?" he asked. "There – coming up from the Antarctic Peninsula. Ah, it's beautiful. You're not even looking."

She groaned, turning in the bed, pulling the sheet up over her shoulder.

"Mess," he whispered, "watch it with me."

She felt his hand, gentle, urging, upon her hip for a moment and, sighing, turned and propped herself up on her elbow, rubbing her eye with her fist. The great, wide, gaping window-wall of their berth rose up before her. He was sitting naked on the edge of the bed in front of it, the Earth-light bathing his eager face in its singular, greenish glow, and he was beckoning to her over his shoulder. Slowly, groggily, she slipped over to the edge of the bed beside him, feeling the cool air upon her own bare skin.

Gazing down through the thick glass, she beheld the spectral, green light of the Aurora Australis shining six hundred miles below. Awe and revulsion, wonder and despair wrestled within her. "I've seen it," she said, tepidly. "Nothing like it used to be. The colour's all wrong. Certainly not beautiful."

"Yes," he said, firmly, "it is. You just have to look the right way." He pointed through the thick glass. "I bet you've never seen Tierra del Fuego look any better than that."

A reluctant smile came to her lips. "The Land of Green Fire," she murmured, languidly.

"Yes! Now you are beginning to see properly. Green fire is still fire. You just have to *see* it."

"But the world is still sick," she whispered. She felt an icy finger slip down her spine and she shivered, wrapping the sheet around herself. "No matter how you look at it. Sick and dying."

"No," he said, again with that firmness that she had never before heard in him. She looked over at him and saw him shaking his head, saw the fervour in his eyes, in the Earth's eerie light. "As long as we still keep going, keep trying, she will always be here, waiting for us to save her. We are her children. She is our mother. We owe it to her and to ourselves."

She reached out and gently slid her hand across his back, brushing his broad shoulders with her finger-tips. "What if she needs more than us?" she asked, "What if she needs a miracle? I don't know if I believe in them anymore."

"What's out there, just beyond orbit? *That* is our miracle. Your father's key....."

She leant the side of her face on his shoulder. "What will I do after you leave tomorrow?" she murmured. "Who will be alive for me then? Who will believe in the new, hopeful future then?"

He turned to face her. "You will. But....." His eyes darted back to the window. "There is something else," he said in a hushed voice, "that will stay behind. With you. Something from an idea that Idris had." He hesitated, darting his eyes back to hers, and then shrugged. "A piece of me that you may find helpful. In case -"

She laid a finger over his lips and shook her head. "Don't say anything more. Right now I still have the real thing, don't I? And I'm not about to let it disappear without making sure I've already got something to remember it by." She lay back on the bed and drew him to her.

"Mess," he murmured in her ear, "Mess….."

The tone came again and she realized, with a start, that it had come many times already.

"What?" she said, blinking. She licked her lips. *I've been dreaming. Of Brayton. Back before…..*

"Mess!" came a shout from far away. "Mess! What's happening?"

She sat up in the foam chair, rigid once more.

"Spatial and temporal anomaly isolated," a soft, electronic, female voice was saying. *"Phenomenon opaque to sensory probes. No data available."*

Slowly, with difficulty, she focussed her eyes upon the screen before her, at the flashing image in red in its exact centre. "That's the planet," she murmured, frowning. "Or moon or whatever the hell this place is. And that other shape is…..Oh, my God," she breathed, "It's the Doorway…..it's not in the Mountain at all….." She turned within her chair. "Brayton!" She struggled to get up, to rise. "Brayton! It's the Portal….."

That was when the ship died.

The vid-screen went dark, the panels switched off, their lights snuffed out like so many tiny stars winking out of existence all around her. The hum beneath her chair, the thrumming running through her body, ceased. Everything ceased. Everything ended.

There was nothing.

She sat there, dumb, open-mouthed. *No more power.*

A hoarse cry escaped her lips, no more than a groan. "Power," she croaked, still sitting in the chair, enfolded once more in the wavering, blue light coming through the cock-pit windows, "Of course! How stupid! The power is gone. That's what you wanted me to do. Wake it up, turn it on. It was all a lie! *Bastard!*"

But there was only the silence around her now. Deep. Utter. As if it were only her and the wavering, blue light in all the universe. Her and *It*.

She no longer sensed Brayton outside.

"Brayton?" she called but her voice caught in her throat. She tried again. *"Brayton?"*

A deep tremor shook her in her contoured chair, shook the entire chamber of rock in which her tiny ship perched upon its pedestal, but there was no reply from outside. Once again, she struggled to get up, to exit the enormous seat and this time, unsteadily, succeeded.

Once on her feet, however, she realized how weak she had become. In the midst of surging rage and fear, she felt it. So weak and spent. Her head swam again and she tottered on her feet. She had to grip the head-rest to steady herself and keep from swooning.

Again, It has me dehydrated and under-nourished. Again, It has me right where It wants me.

She had no weapon and no supplies – only her coveralls, somewhere her suit, and her wits. And – she patted her breast pocket and felt the tiny device within it. "And this," she mumbled, bewildered. She drew out the micro-labe and looked down at it in her palm uncertainly.

It seemed to waver in her hand.

But it could have been the pulsing, blue light entering in through the cock-pit bubble.

You still won't see it, will you? Look again!

"No!" she screamed, "Leave me alone!" She curled her fist around the device. Or whatever it was.

The machine on the table, the box in the cavern, this? They're all the same bloody thing? Yes. I can feel it. But what? Why can't I see it?

"I got you the power from my ship," she shouted, "I gave you everything. What more do you want from me? Just *take* it!"

Then It was gone again. Her mind was free once more.

She slumped, leaning over the head-rest of the chair, defeated. For a time she sobbed quietly. She did not know for how long.

Then, slowly, she stood up straight again. Quietly, calmly, she stepped forward and dismounted the steps leading out of the hatch. And left *Beta One* for the last time.

XI

Black-out.

Why is it dark? What happened to the rock-light?
She flailed her hands out before her, passed them in front of her face, but there was nothing there and nothing to see. And then there was a flicker.
Not blue. Fluorescent lighting. She groaned. *Another carnival ride?* Tentatively, she stuck out a foot and felt solid flooring. She was not at the top of a rocky stage with a tiny, inter-galactic spaceship sitting behind her. *That* much was clear. She took in a ragged breath and tried to brace herself for what might come next and then stepped forward again. Abruptly, she realized that she was no longer wearing her Syndicate-issued boots but rather soft-soled, comfortably-fitting shoes. *Ones made for walking, walking all day…..Personally-engineered….. Ones I haven't worn since…..*

Her heart gave a lurch but she dared not allow the thought that tried to force its way into her conscious mind to move to its logical conclusion.

Instead, seeing a doorway now, the far side of which shone with the un-mistakable, flickering, sickly-hued, utilitarian lighting, she passed through it into a narrow hallway. She blinked, looking around her. Her heart leapt into her throat and beads of sweat stood out on her skin.

A sign on the white, poly-vinyl wall across from her: *Level 4.*

Her head began to spin. "No, I'm not here. I'm not back," she said but her voice sounded distant, muted.

Yet the question was no longer where she was. It was *when*. Again, the spectre in her mind rose up and she forced it desperately down again. The throbbing of her heart seemed louder in her own ears than her dampened voice had been.

Slowly exhaling, she turned and began to step quickly along the thin, worn carpet of the hallway, turning her head from side to side, seeing, verifying, yet knowing it was all there, all set up, complete. Her heart hammered within her chest.

The klaxon began to sound somewhere down the corridor, short and metallic, and red panel lights in the walls began to flicker. She froze. *And so it begins.*

She began to run.

"Mariss!" called a voice, distant, dull, "Mariss! Come quick! It's out of control!"

A face, a girl, swam before her eyes, standing in front of her in the corridor, flailing blue-uniformed arms.

"Daniela," Mariss said, mechanically, feeling it now, the whole awful weight of it, knowing it had to be played out, had to be gone through to its bitter end, "what's going on?"

"The supply ship, the drone," the girl was babbling breathlessly, yet distantly, face hidden, even though she was standing directly before her, blocking her way, "from Earth - it's lost its attitude control and won't make the port. It'll slam into the Module!"

Mariss, numb, could only slowly shake her head.

The girl grabbed her left arm and yanked her hard and now she registered at last the presence of the hand-book in her left hand.

She opened her mouth to scream but nothing came out.

She was not playing it right.

And so she ran, letting the girl pull her along the hallway, the klaxon still screaming, her left hand still clutching *Dimensions of Hyper-Spatial Forms*.

Now other figures, other men and women, appeared around them, faint and ghost-like, all of them running yet the only sound was the siren, the damned siren that always filled her dreams – she could remember that now – had always haunted her sleep.....*before*.

She was lagging.

Daniela had long since given up her arm and she and the others had surged ahead to the viewing area but her own legs as she ran had begun to feel like thin, iron bands; they shook and wobbled perilously beneath her. She could no longer run but only stagger along after them.

Ahead, where they had stampeded around a turn to the left, there was a dark corner on the right, and, her chest a bleak, black pit now, she lurched inexorably toward it.

Please. Please, no.

In a flash, from the blackness, something came at her.

She felt a painful, iron grip upon her right arm, as if it were seized in a vise, and she was wrenched around and hurtled against the corridor wall within the darkened cul-de-sac with a force so brutal it knocked the air from her lungs.

A hand, damp with sweat, clamped itself tightly over her mouth while the forearm of the opposite arm rammed itself hard into her throat and held there, almost cutting off all air to her lungs and all blood to her head. Dimly, she could feel a leg crammed up against and over her thighs, utterly pinning her to the wall.

From here on in, she would only listen. And feel. And try to endure.

"Marisseena," panted a voice in her ear. There was a shadow standing before her, right against her in fact, there in the darkness, but it had no face. "I think I understand human power better now. It is different…..from that of machines."

Yes, she could only listen…..

…..but no longer understand. The shadow had the same voice, the same clipped, accented voice, but now *it* was not playing it right.

"The other one, the one who…..*loves*…..you," said the shadow in her ear, enunciating its words carefully, "he was my favourite before you came. He began to teach me…..about emotions…..that they had power in themselves. *Your* power."

She could scarcely see the dark form there in front of her, could scarcely hear it.

"This love that he calls it, this bond," muttered the shadow, its hand still clamped over her mouth, its arm still over her throat, "…..now that you are here I know it better, I *feel* its power better."

She listened even though, just as it always did at this point, her head began to swim as the oxygen decreased and she knew that unconsciousness would soon follow.

Yet, desperately, she tried to follow what this shadow was saying, for these words had never come before; they were apart.

"And with the one you call 'Sister'," it grunted in her ear, "ahh, now that is a different form, yes. That is a *strong* feel, that one. I had known…..pain before. But no. This pain. It is beyond. It is…..deep."

Then everything intensified. The hand clamped tighter so that it seemed it would break her teeth within her mouth and the arm across her throat - it seemed to cut clear through to the back of her skull.

Her eyes rolled back in their sockets.

"But this one," the voice hissed, now far, far away, "now that you are here - your living, breathing presence - this one is more than any other power I have ever tasted before. What is it called? What *is* it?"

Dimly, distantly, she somehow felt him release her crushed throat with his arm and begin to paw at her breasts with his hand.

The note-book, -

Dimensions of Hyper-Spatial Forms. Yes.

- the note-book with the warped, wire ring-binding and the small, bent, twin metal prongs sticking out on its spine, rose in her left hand of its own accord.

She had just felt him touch something in her breast-pocket when the notebook struck him full in the face like a thunder-clap.

In the darkness, she saw it. Miraculously, she seemed to recover her senses and see it. There was only a wavering, blue light all around them now.

And Leo Ilsudov, his cheek slashed to bloody ribbons, screamed as he always did.

Only this time it was not him.

XII

The scream went on and on, filling her ears and her brain. She felt strong arms assailing her and she tried to fight them off, tried to push them away from her.

"Mariss! Mariss!"

With a start, she realized that the screams were her own. They were pouring forth from her lips like a gushing torrent, unstoppable, filling the air around her, the cool, echoing air.

"Mariss, please! Remember what I told you."

She clamped her mouth shut.

The shrill, piercing cries were cut off and she looked up with wild, bulging eyes, into the face of her ancient husband again, the one on whom somehow untold years had descended and who was kneeling beside her, bending over her. Around her was his cavern and beneath her his stone-bed.

My God, how long have I been here? It seems like years.

Maybe it has been.

She watched him let out a long, tortured breath, and saw that the inane, blank expression that had seemed etched on his face before was now no longer there but rather, in its place, a hidden spark, a concealed empathy – a humanity - dwelt. *A connection?*

Yet, a terror clutched at her with razor-sharp talons and she could not dwell on it. The dread weight of her own doom was crushing her. She began to weep. "Oh, Brayton," she groaned, and she felt the tears trace scalding tracks across her cheeks, "It got you. From all the others. It tired of all the rest but kept you. To feed off you. All these years…..for so many years. I thought you were a dream too, a nightmare. I don't know how it has been so long. And now it's got me too. We're never going to get out of here, are we? Never."

His softened gaze did not leave hers and his withered, though strong, hand brushed, awkwardly, at her hair. "Shhh," he whispered, brokenly. "Rest."

She swallowed, looking up at him through her tears. "I don't know all that you have suffered," she said, in a trembling voice, "but I'm beginning to understand it." She brought a shaking hand to the side of her head. "The shock and the trauma. It's messed with your head too. You've forgotten everything. Even me. But that's okay." She reached out and laid her hand on his and he drew in a quick breath at her touch. "Maybe…..we can get to know each other again. Maybe we can start over."

Open-mouthed, he stared down at her hand - now grasping his.

Abruptly, he lurched to his feet, taking his arm from her, and turned away. She watched, bewildered, as he stood, tottering, his back to her. Then she swallowed painfully again. Her throat was dry and constricted and throbbing. *There was truth in the nightmare this time. Reality in the dream.* Rubbing delicately at her throat with one hand, she slowly sat up in the hard bed and wiped her eyes with the back of the other. *It was changing, morphing into reality. It will drive me mad, just like it did him.*

"I'm terribly weak," she said, "Is there anything - ?"

With a shiver, Brayton stepped precariously across the cavern, his white, silk-like robe flowing behind him. She watched him go to the far wall near a stone shelf upon which sat a shining, blue lamp and hunker down before the open, black hole that still gaped there.

"I think I've learned how to block It," she whispered to his back, hearing her words hiss amongst the rock walls and between the rock ceiling and floor. "I can teach you how. But I need your help too."

He paused for an instant and then reached out and grasped the white box hidden within the dark hole. Stiffly, he rose and turned toward her, the box nestled within his arms. "Yes," he said, thickly, "It is time to refresh and revive yourself now." He cleared his throat. "You are right. You are weak and in distress."

There was a silence between them, between all of the rock walls of the cavern, the stone ceiling, the floor.

Slowly, he moved toward her, holding the box before him and she could see that it was still covered by the same, soft, white material. Swallowing painfully again, she took it from his hands, reached for the covering and, unhesitatingly, flung it aside.

It was there.

She looked sideways at him and saw that he was staring down at it, uncomprehendingly.

"Now," she said, quietly, returning her own gaze to the tiny device inside the box. She swallowed yet again, wincing, trying to brace herself, "listen to my voice and do everything I say. I'm going to ask you to.....look at me and concentrate only on me. Think about.....think about your love for me. Nothing else."

She felt him tremble but he did not speak. Slowly, she looked up at him, still standing before her. His blue eyes were now fastened upon hers.

"There is a way," she said, daring to press him. "It can be beaten. But you are expendable now. Do you understand what I say? It no longer needs you to get what It wants. This only I can do for It now." Keeping her eyes on his, she took the micro-labe in her hand and lifted it from the box. "This is what

It wants now, why It can't hurt me. Yet. But *I need you* to help me to see it properly."

He remained quiet and she dared not turn her eyes from his. Not yet. There was too much at stake.

"Okay?" she said, swallowing. "When you concentrate on me you make a shield of your mind." She felt her heart beat faster. *We may do this. But what chance do we really have?* "I need to see this the right way." She curled her fist around the small device in her hand. "For some reason my mind has been…..hurt and has become fixed on this. Perhaps because it is the nearest thing to what it really is. But I think you can help me to see it…..for real." She took in a breath. *Now for it.*

"It can help us escape," she whispered, "Now take my hand. We will have more power that way. And call for Zenya."

XIII

The spark vanished from his eyes. They became veiled once again; lifeless.

She lashed out her hand and grabbed his. "No! Look at me! Don't lose me." The eyes blinked and re-focussed on her. "Teach me! Teach me about Zenya! It's the only way."

A long, agonized groan burst from his lips. Then he wrenched his arm from her grasp and raised shaking hands toward her. His withered, wrinkled face contorted as if he were suffering excruciating pain deep within his very soul and she could only watch him helplessly.

"What's happening?" she murmured.

Her heart leapt into her throat. A blue glow softly kindled in his hands.

"Not 'Zenya'!" he snapped, making her jump, "Zhe -"

The Creature stood amongst them. There was no warning. If Mariss found that she could now sense Its presence if she tried with every fibre of her being, or could enter Its mind if she tried hard enough, just as It could hers, these truths were not yet known to her. It still bore the form and stature and countenance of her long-dead sister – even, somehow hideously now, still bore the flannel onesie with the brown teddy-bears on it - and Its face, the face which un-naturally enhanced and yet irredeemably marred the beauty of that of Solea Tusten Arlen, was darkened as by a deep, black shadow. Its lime-yellow eyes, Mariss Arlen Keppeler saw, glowed like embers.

In Its own small hands, upraised and blazing, was a blue fire that far exceeded that of her husband.

In her seven-year-old sister's voice, It screamed, "No!"

Then rocks and stones were pelting her, striking her in the head, in the face. She was aware of warm, tacky blood on her cheek. The very bed-rock beneath her feet began to fall away, crumbling into dust. Dust filled the air, filled her lungs, blinded her eyes. And beyond all, above all, and within all, an unbearable roaring suddenly filled her ears and shook her to her very bones.

She began to fall into an abyss.

"Take her!" Solea's voice shrieked within the haze, amidst the ruin, inside her head. Somehow, distantly, she felt powerful arms coil around her even though she seemed incorporeal now, without substance, without form.

The Creature spoke the Word, the proper Word, and there was a blinding flash of blue.

Blessed peace came.

XIV

"One more touch."
"We should go. Now."
"It's God in here!"
"Breathe. You must breathe."

Yes?
She breathed.

Not too fast. Do not breathe too fast.

Slowly, eyes closed, she filled her lungs with blessed oxygen, held it, and then slowly exhaled. Her breath sounded in her ears; an enormous sound. It filled her head. So too did the beating of her heart. Only gradually, did they slow.
She opened her eyes.

The sun was setting.

I can no longer bring the oxygen. The Mountain is gone.

She saw it through the tinted visor of her helmet. Even at that moment, its huge disk was touching the world, its eerie, waning, cobalt rays radiating through a swiftly-darkening sky.

There is no other place.

"I am not dead," she said, carefully, measuredly, into her helmet mic, and her words filled her head even as her breath and her heart-beat. The distant, azure sun bathed her in its quickly-fading light.

Your power remains but it is weakening.

"But where am I? Where have you brought me?"
The deep, blue disk was half-gone. Slowly, it ebbed until it was only a dull arc.

To Zhen-Yah.

Below her, far, far below, a dust eddy arose. She watched it for a time as its faint form swirled before the dying sun. She stood upon a lip of stone within the throat of an enormous cave set high in a chain of strange, twisted, black hills. At their feet the blue desert stretched as far as she could see; even as far as that huge, blue disk itself.
There was nothing else beneath the yawning, indigo sky.

Her breath came and went in her ears, came and went.

"And where is Brayton?"

The dulled, blue sun slipped beneath the blue sands and the eddy blew across the dust.

"I said, 'Where is Brayton?'"

All warmth fled.

XV

She staggered through the maw of the cave. Behind her, night had fallen over the strange, harsh world and a cold like she had never before known grasped at her with icy fingers. She could hear the temperature stabilizers whining within her suit, trying to keep it away. Within the threshold, with trembling, gloved hands, she switched on her helmet-lamp and its thin, pencil-beam of white light stabbed through the dimness before her. Above, there was only blackness and ahead the same. Only the floor and the giant maw itself gave any indication of space, of something other than nothing.

(A red warning upon the inside of her visor: 30 minutes of oxygen reserve remaining.)

Her foot slipped over a loose rock on the cave floor and now her breath was coming faster in spite of every warning she could give herself to slow it down, to conserve it.

And she thought that the Creature knew her peril now; how very close to death she was.

"Talk to me," she said, shakily, into the helmet mic, pausing upon the cave floor amidst the strewn rocks and stones. "I know you do not want me to die. I can still help you. Even now."

She waited, trying to slow her breath. There was no answer.

Reluctantly, she moved deeper into the cave even though for her now there was nowhere left to go.

Come on....I know you're there. Talk to me.

She drew up short, gasping. The girl – the Creature – her sister's shade - stood not a meter before her, perched atop a kind of conical, grey, dirt-covered rampart with her small, padded feet planted upon its jagged rim. She was cocking her head at her.

"Why do you look like her all the time?" Mariss snapped, in spite of herself, "To torment me? To drive me crazy? I know you do not need to."

No. But you are here. You make it easiest.

A blue aura surrounded the girl as the voice came inside her head and she stared through her visor. *You mean it's easiest to feed off me, even when I'm dying.*

"I can help you," Mariss repeated, trying to collect herself, trying to remain calm, yet she heard her own breath begin to wheeze through the helmet mic, "but you must help me now. I need -"

I will show you.

The girl vanished from atop the rampart. Just as suddenly Mariss spotted her scampering swiftly across the debris-covered floor. Mariss, panting, not speaking, began to stumble after her.

Here.
(Oxygen supply – 20 minutes.)

The girl, limned in blue fire, stood beside an open mouth in the side of a large, irregular, sprawling mound upon the cave floor. Mariss panned her dimming helmet lamp all along its surface but there were no discernible features to it, only a formless grey mass. "What is this?" she murmured.

The girl cocked her head at her. ***The place of the others.***

Mariss blew out a long breath and took in another. Carefully, she stepped through the opening in the side of the mound. The dimness clung here too and yet vague walls showed themselves. They were strikingly straight and flat, yet indiscernible like everything else. *Made?* Platforms of what appeared to be grey rock stood in rows along the walls on either hand, but they were smooth, bevelled. Dust lay everywhere. Her breath increased. "What am I looking at?" she whispered.

The others came to the far side. Like you. Far from Zhen-Yah. But Zhen-Yah showed me. Zhen-Yah showed me the water inside the Mountain

where the oxygen was and increased the tunnels. To help you and them not die; to save your power.

Giving out another sharp breath, Mariss panned her helmet-lamp along the nearest platform of stone and then stepped carefully toward it. She reached out a gloved hand and ran it slowly through the dust that lay upon it.

Something began to gnaw at the inside of her stomach.

Layers upon layers of dust lay upon this platform, just as it lay upon all the others, and suddenly she was gouging at it with her fingers, her breath filling her ears, until at last she uncovered a dull, opaque surface. Drawing yet closer, she peered down at it, breathlessly, her lamp bathing it in its dying light.

Her breath caught in her throat.

"Space Goo." She managed it at last in a flat voice and it echoed inside her head as if it were itself a cave. "Space Goo. Like what was covering my legs. Like what I carried with me. Like what *Alpha* carried with her." Fighting for breath, she felt cold fingers slip around her wind-pipe and begin to squeeze. In agony, she brought her hands to her throat.

Five years, maybe six, he said in the dream, in the illusion. But this…..no…..not fifty or sixty…..not even five hundred…..

Her knees buckled beneath her and she fell hard upon them on the dusty floor. She opened her mouth to scream.

Wait. STOP.

She clutched, desperately, at her helmet with her gloved hands and slowly the cold fingers slipped their icy grasp from her throat.

Zhen-Yah keeps all things. Zhen-Yah remembers. Zhen-Yah does not forget.

Shaking, hollow all over, she looked up. There before her, next to the girl, in the doorway of the grey chamber, stood the crew of *Alpha*.
She gasped, feebly.
She saw Dallicet Olenas and Wahlia Deepa. She saw John Naishen and the unknown man. She saw Leo and Larissa Ilsudov. She saw their little girl. They were in their uniforms - all except the girl, who had kept her dress - as if on duty, yet they were be-grimed, wasted, un-kempt. Their faces were barren, their eyes blank. And they saw her.
Slowly, one by one, in utter silence, they began to step past her - still on her knees upon the dust-covered floor - glancing down at her vacantly as they passed. The little girl's veiled eyes sent a shiver down her back. *Are they in spirit? In hallucination? Are they in body only?* She watched as they slowly and purposefully walked along the rows of dust-caked stone plinths and now she knew that they were not stone plinths at all but rather sleep pods. And she knew something else.
It's the Alpha. *I'm kneeling inside the sleep-chamber of* Alpha.

XVI

She watched, barely registering, as the centuries-old walls began to suffuse with blue light, the light of **Zhen-Yah.**

"You brought them here." Slowly, she struggled to her feet, head reeling, and found that she could not turn her gaze from them - from the fated crew - even for a moment. Her breath rattled in her ears. *I found you. I came for you. But I was too late. Far, far too late. I'm sorry. I'm so sorry.* "You brought them here…..after. Didn't you?"

There is no other place.

They stood at the heads of their sleep pods. Waiting. The little girl stood with her mother.

"Are they now only shadows?'

These that you see are the images of what has been. What has been has been kept. What has been kept will not be lost.

She trembled. "And so you have brought me too. Here. To…..keep me."

The form and essence of your power will be preserved. It will remain. With Zhen-Yah.

(Oxygen supply – 10 minutes.)

"But where," she said, quietly, and now she no longer panted or heard her own breath in her ears. The faces of the crew seemed to glisten as she spoke, "where is Brayton? My husband. Is he not also…..kept? Has he not also remained?"

Then, suddenly, he was there, standing within the open bay of the long-dead ship.
She cried out. He wore no uniform, had no sign of rank, merely stood as an old man, stooped, in white robes. Yet, he was not staring at her blankly as had the others. He *knew* her. She could see it in his eyes.
She lurched toward him. He held out to her in his bony hand a tiny object.

This one my friend, from the beginning. Awakened from Zhen-Yah. Taken over that form which I choose, which pleases me most. Who remains with me. Until he returns.

She reached for the object in Brayton's hand only somehow it was not him, not her husband. *How can that be? He knows me. He loves me.*

And I him.

She took it in her glove and as she did so he grasped her hand.

She saw it clearly at last.

Then he was gone, moving steadily and purposefully toward the head of the last remaining pod, his robe hanging limply from his thin shoulders.

Out of the corner of her eye, she saw the Creature jerk Its hands into the air. Startled, she turned to watch It scamper after him on Its small, padded feet. There was surprise in Its green-yellow eyes and Its small mouth was open

(It did not know this was going to happen.)

but no voice was coming into her head; Its thoughts were not directed at her.

Old Brayton –

a sudden tremor surged through her. *No, not Old Brayton – Brayton Two…..*

– looked up at her for a moment, ignoring the Creature, and then lifted his hands. In unison with him, the crew of the *Alpha* bent over and placed their hands upon the surfaces of their sleep pods. She watched as the light waxed within their fingers and then spread to engulf both bodies and pods alike.

They melted away.

And yet Brayton did not, not at first. Instead, as the others diminished, he grew; until he stood tall, even twice his proper height, willowy, and with legs impossibly long and thin.

Her mouth fell open.

And then he too was gone.

What happened? Why was he different? Was he.....one of them?"

Startled, she looked down. The girl, yellow-green eyes gleaming, stood directly before her on the dusty, bay floor.

You sent him back. What did you say to him? Why has he gone?

Trembling all over, her eyes fell to the object in her right hand, at its recessed, plasteel grips and its dark face. She reached a shaking left hand and adjusted her helmet mic frequency on her sleeve.

"Brayton Two," she said, unevenly, "Ident Mariss."

A row of green lights blinked upon the dark face of the palm-comp in her hand and then shone steadily.

"Long time, Mess," said a voice in her ears and she gave out a small sob at its sound, *"I was starting to worry. Do you want me to power up?"*

Tell me. What did you say?

"No," she gasped, "Only rudimentary functions for now. I need a location of a power source. It's urgent."

Tell me.
Please.

"One seven five meters. Your ten o'clock. A big one. Your voice harmonics are un-stable, Mess, are you sure you don't want me at full power?"

"Only when I say. Stand-By."

"Check."

She glanced up from the palm-comp. The girl was peering, curiously, down at it in her hand now and she felt Its thoughts turned aside from her. Then the strange eyes returned; the cocked head.

Teach me the sounds. What do they mean?

Purposely blocking her mind, Mariss began to walk in the direction of the power source, pushing the Creature out of the way. She felt It probing her, felt Its urgency. It was not pushing her, not yet – evidently her value was still too high to repeat messy extractions - yet she could feel Its vast strength even so.

Everything rides on controlling your own thoughts right now, Honey. You're shoving all your chips into the middle of the table here. You're all in. No more deals after this one.

(Oxygen supply: 5 minutes)

There had been a faint glow in the direction she had been walking and now there could be no mistaking it.

She stood, fully wheezing now, before the cave wall itself, basking within the crack of a brilliant, blue light that assaulted her tinted visor.

Have you come to see?

She gave a jerk. The Creature had been silent the whole way, retreating from the barrier of her thoughts, and even now was standing off from her right elbow, almost deferentially. For the moment, she dared put It off yet further and tilted her head back, trying to see the top of the cave wall that rose up, towering, above her. Its lofty heights were lost in the gloom. Her helmet-lamp was now too dim to serve any useful purpose in any case and her head, as she leant it back, was seized with a wave of vertigo, making her stumble backward. Her straining breath in her ears now seemed a part of the new reality as if it had always been.

Throughout, the girl-shade merely watched her.

It is not forbidden. You will not be harmed.

"Brayton, talk to me," Mariss gasped.

"Your power source is a big one, Mess. Ten meters beyond this wall. Preliminary indications show that its incandescent properties alone approach stellar phenomena."

"That's not possible," she murmured.

Then the crack of light was expanding and she staggered back from it.

The Creature remained where It was, Its small face bathed in the dazzling light. Slowly, It raised an arm toward it.

"I can't get a proper reading on its energy output, it's shielded somehow," Brayton Two was saying in her ears, *"Extremely powerful, though."*

She felt her own eyes fasten upon the light streaming through the ever-widening crack in the cave wall. She should not be able to endure it, even through the visor, yet somehow she was.

"Wait…..there's something unusual about its power….."

The Creature was turning toward her, head tilted, eyes shining. Into her own head, despite all of the mental defences she thought she had built within it, exploded a word and it sent a terrifying jolt through her entire body. She knew what it was the instant before it came:

ZHEN-YAH.

Wincing, her hands at the sides of her helmet, she groaned, "It's joined. It's joined to the Portal, isn't it? You're seeing the flux of the two sources; feeding off one another."

"Correct, Mess. I detect two energy sources; the one situated upon the surface, contained and shielded here, and the other an enormous torus surrounding the entire planet. There is a corridor of pure energy passing between them but it's not two-way. The one in orbit is feeding this one."

(Oxygen supply – 2 minutes)

Her breath filled her ears. "My God," she gasped, "that has to be it." She stumbled a few paces farther from the open crack through which the blue light flooded and turned and beheld it again.

"Come again, Mess. What has to be it?"

The opening stretched tall and wide before her, its straight, uniform edges sharp in relief against the light.

"Mess?"

"It's a chamber," she croaked, "for a drive engine." She turned her head, trying to search all of the vast, darkened cave surrounding her, the lost depths and heights. "With an alien power source we don't understand enhanced by the Portal. This whole, god-damned thing…..it's a *ship*."

The last was only a whisper.

She found herself staggering toward the Creature. It merely watched her curiously as she came on. She forced herself to look into Its unnerving, limpid eyes. Its head was still tilted at her. "You came here too, you Bitch," she gasped, "millennia, eons ago, who knows?" Everything was wavering before her now. "Your engine's drive did it, caught you here like a fly on fly-paper. Maybe you had a crew too and you're all that's left. You're trapped here just like me, just like us."

She laughed. She actually laughed, a weak, torpid, ghastly sound.

(Oxygen supply – one minute. Please get to nearest emergency closet immediately. One minute of oxygen remaining.)

I do not understand.

"It means if there is a way in….." she shook a gloved finger in the Creature's face, "…..there is a way out." Her breath was grating now, her lungs beginning to burn. "Brayton," she gasped, "it's likely the energy source of the engine created the singularity in the first place, maybe even when nearing this blue star. It's an interstitial tear. Self-sustaining. Somehow it found us, sent out worm-holes to us through Space." She felt herself swooning. Desperately, she tried to keep conscious.

There was a pause. She could sense the Creature regarding her silently, Its thoughts quiescent. It returned Its gaze to the light.

"You mean like a space between Spaces, a time between Times," said Brayton Two in her ears.

"Yes," she whispered, "exactly. If it's a flow, it can be reversed. From the engine to the Doorway, and then beyond to the other side. You have the Key."

"Your father's tachyon array was adapted into my design, yes, but Mess I do not have the power to inject it into this stream. It's too great. You know that."

Her head was swimming in earnest now. Her lungs were searing and the air within the suit was taking on an acrid tang.

"I need you at full power now," she panted, "Authorization code. …. *Beta Tau Four Zero One.*"

The plasteel face of the comp gleamed at her, adding its own incandescence to that of the alien engine – or what it had become - and she felt its vibrations through her glove.

The Creature whirled its head toward her, eyes hungry.

"You will have the power very soon, Brayton," she rasped, feeling her strength fly away, "Just be ready to inject the stream. You'll know."

"There is no proof that it can be reversed, only expanded, accessed. If you return to the previous Space it may not be the previous Time – or vice….."

"No choice," she croaked and she stumbled amongst the stones and dust of the hard, rock floor of the giant cave.

If that's what it really was.

Oh, God…..

It slipped away. Her life. She could feel Death peering down at her out of the darkness.

With every last ounce of strength, she reached her hand toward the Creature.

And opened her mind to It at last.

XVII

The sounds. Listen to the sounds. Do you hear?

Yes.

Do you understand?

Yes.

Are you touching me? The Object?

Yes.

Then we have done all that we can. Now I must…..rest.

EPILOGUE

She knelt on the cushion and looked out of the window at the grey sky and the rain, pressing her face to the glass. The fat drops were hitting the tarmac like little water-balloons exploding all over its smooth surface. She could see little rivers running down all over and even underneath the fat ship as it sat waiting in its cradle in the middle of the pad. She wondered if it was sad.

"You know, a hundred years ago they had to wait for the rain to stop before they could launch." Her father came and sat down on the long cushion beside her with a sigh. She could catch his faint leathery smell. "It's because in those days they didn't have the ion shielding on the hull that could -"

"Do you think it's sad?"

"What?" he asked, surprised. She turned to see the surprise in his brown eyes.

"I think it's sad. It doesn't want us to go."

He laughed, the great, big laugh that came from his belly. "I suppose if I was stuck out in the rain I wouldn't be *too* happy either but you know what?" He raised an arm toward her. "Come here."

She sat back on her heels and then sprang into his lap, throwing her arms around him.

"Oof!" he grunted, "I wasn't quite ready for *that* launch. But what I was going to say is I'd still be a little bit happy because I'd know I was helping to take families to Mars and helping the families on Earth by doing it."

She hugged him, smelling his leather jacket. She liked it much better than the ratty coveralls that hung up in the lab. Releasing her arms, she sat back in his lap and looked up at him.

"How happy would you be?" she asked him.

He raised his thumb and fore-finger and held them a centimeter apart. "That happy."

She frowned. "That's all?"

"Well, I suppose maybe *this* happy!" And he spread his arms wide and then grabbed her in a huge bear-hug. She squealed with delight and hugged him back, letting his musky smell wash over her.

"But are you really coming?" she murmured against his jacket, "Really, really coming with us? You're not going to stay?"

"Why on Earth would I not come with you, Marisseena," he exclaimed, "Why do you say that?" She could hear the hurt in his voice and she hugged him harder because that was the last thing she wanted to make him feel. But the fear was there more than ever. And that's what *she* was feeling. "I don't know," she said, frowning.

"Listen." He drew apart from her but held her shoulders, looking down into her eyes. "I said no. You know that. Mom knows that. Solea knows that. They wanted me to do more research on the viability of hyper-spatial travel but because *Aries* has grown by leaps and bounds -" he motioned with his hands up and down and she laughed in spite of the fear "– I…..said…..no. Okay?"

She nodded.

"Besides, I think Newton can deal with the W.C. better than I can. And he's welcome to it. Ah, here they are -" he made as if to stand up and she scrambled off of his lap.

While Daddy was standing, talking to Mom, her sister came up to her, holding a small, plastic bag.

"Do you have your ticket?" she asked but Solea shook her head.

"Mom kept it," her sister said.

"But you saw what it says on it?"

Solea nodded. *"Proteus V – Mars."*

"But that one out there isn't it," said Mariss, pointing out the window behind her. "It just gets us up to the Network."

Her sister shrugged, bored. She was never interested in space or space-ships or Daddy's work.

That's why Mariss gasped in delight when she suddenly drew out a tiny model from the bag she was holding.

"Oh! *That's* the *Proteus V! That's* what's taking us to Mars!"

"Mom got it at the gift store and I already took it out of its package. Here." Solea offered it to her and she reached for it, taking it eagerly.

"Thanks," she murmured, happily. Solea shrugged again.

They lifted off in the shuttle, belted down tight in the huge, cushioned chairs. She felt the deep vibrations beneath her just like Daddy had warned her before-hand and she hung on and waited for them to clear the atmosphere when she knew they would stop. They finally did. Taking a deep breath, then – also what Daddy had told her she should do – she looked across the narrow aisle. She and Daddy were on one side of the small ship and Solea and Mom were on the other. Right now, the both of them seemed to be sleeping peacefully across the way.

Daddy touched her arm. "We'll be at the Port on the Net in thirty minutes," he said, "Then we'll dock."

"Is that the big knock?" she said, somewhat anxiously.

"Hmm?" he said, "Oh…..when we clamp on. Yes. A little. But nothing to worry about." He smiled down at her. Nervously, she drew out the model of the *Proteus* again and began to look at it carefully to see if it was broken. For some reason she thought it had been.

"Something happened to it," she muttered, examining it but it was new and un-harmed.

"Can I see?"

Startled, she turned to see her sister staring hard at the little ship in her hand, her emerald-green eyes keen. She had never seen Solea look so hard at anything space-related before and, wordlessly, she handed the model across the aisle to her.

"It's not right," her sister said, looking down at it intently. "It's – *ohh!*"

She dropped it.

Only, in the zero g it merely drifted slowly away from her startled face.

Mariss had seen it too, however, and her heart was in her throat.

Even now, the soft, blue glow was lingering upon the tiny *Proteus V.*

And upon her sister's trembling finger-tips.

www.ingramcontent.com/pod-product-compliance
Lightning Source LLC
LaVergne TN
LVHW091557060526
838200LV00036B/877